Elsie's Winter Trip

The Original Elsie Classics

Elsie Dinsmore
Elsie's Holidays at Roselands
Elsie's Girlhood
Elsie's Womanhood
Elsie's Motherhood
Elsie's Children
Elsie's Widowhood
Grandmother Elsie
Elsie's New Relations
Elsie at Nantucket
The Two Elsies
Elsie's Kith and Kin
Elsie's Friends at Woodburn
Christmas with Grandma Elsie
Elsie and the Raymonds
Elsie Yachting with the Raymonds
Elsie's Vacation
Elsie at Viamede
Elsie at Ion
Elsie at the World's Fair
Elsie's Journey on Inland Waters
Elsie at Home
Elsie on the Hudson
Elsie in the South
Elsie's Young Folks
Elsie's Winter Trip
Elsie and Her Loved Ones
Elsie and Her Namesakes

Elsie's Winter Trip

Book Twenty-Six of
The Original Elsie Classics

Martha Finley

CUMBERLAND HOUSE
NASHVILLE, TENNESSEE

Elsie's Winter Trip
by Martha Finley

Any unique characteristics of this edition:
Copyright © 2001 by Cumberland House Publishing, Inc.

Published by Cumberland House Publishing, Inc.,
431 Harding Industrial Drive, Nashville, Tennessee 37211.

Cover design by Bruce Gore, Gore Studios, Inc.
Photography by Dean Dixon Photography
Hair and Makeup by Calene Rader
Text design by Heather Armstrong

Printed in the United States of America
1 2 3 4 5 6 7 8 — 05 04 03 02 01

CHAPTER FIRST

"LU, DEAR, CAN YOU possibly give me an early breakfast tomorrow morning?" asked Chester, as they made their preparations for retiring that first night in their new home.

"I think so," she returned, giving him a wifely look and smile. "How early would you like to have it?"

"About seven, I think. I've told our coachman, Jack, that I want the carriage at eight. He will drive me into town and then return, so that both carriage and horses will be ready at a reasonably early hour for its other three owners — our brother and sister and yourself."

"It was certainly very kind and thoughtful of you to give such an order," she said with a smile, "but we would much prefer to have your company in all our drives and visits."

"I should very much like to give it to you. But there is business that should have been attended to some time ago, and I must not be longer delayed in attending to it."

"If it is, it shall not be your wife's fault," she replied. "The cook is still in the kitchen, and I will go and give my order at once for an early seven o'clock breakfast."

"Lu, dear," Chester said on her return, "it will not be necessary for you to rise in time for so early a breakfast. I can pour my own coffee and eat alone."

"No, you can't have that privilege while I'm your wife," she responded with a saucy look and smile. "I intend to pour your coffee and see that you have an appetizing breakfast and do justice to it."

"Your presence will make it doubly enjoyable, dearest," he returned, putting an arm about her and giving her a look of loving admiration. "But you must not be robbed of your needed rest and sleep."

"Thank you, my dear husband," she replied, "but I am accustomed to early rising, and it agrees with me. Oh, I think I shall greatly enjoy taking an early breakfast with you. Isn't it delightful to begin our married life in so lovely a home of our very own?"

"It is, indeed! And we owe it all to your good, kind, and most generous father."

"He is that, most emphatically," responded Lucilla, "the dearest, best, and kindest father in the world."

Seven o'clock the next morning found them cozily seated at a little round table in their pretty dining room, enjoying a delicious breakfast of fresh fruits, broiled fowl, hot muffins, and coffee. These, added to good health, cheerful spirits, and a fondness for each other's society made them a happy couple.

The meal was enlivened with cheerful chat.

"I am sorry you have to hurry so," Lucilla said, as she filled her husband's cup for the second time. "I really think you ought to have at least a little longer holiday."

"I expect to take it piecemeal, nights and mornings, in the society of my wife," returned Chester with an affectionate look and smile. "I was very glad to get this case," he added, "for if I succeed with it, it will bring me some thousands."

"I shall be glad of that for your sake," said Lucilla. "But don't work too hard. You know you are not very strong. Therefore, you need to take good care of yourself."

"Ah, my dear, be careful how you encourage me in self-indulgence," laughed Chester. "I am too much inclined that way as it is."

"Are you?" she exclaimed with mirthful look and tone. "I really had not found it out but thought you one of the foolishly industrious people who will even throw away health in order to get on rapidly with their work."

"And I," laughed Chester, "took you for a woman of such discernment that you must have found out before this what a lazy, incompetent fellow you have thrown yourself away upon."

"No, with all my discernment I have yet to make that discovery. I did not marry the fellow you describe—but a bright, talented, industrious young man. I won't have him slandered."

At that moment, a servant came in with the announcement that the carriage was at the door.

"Ah! Jack is quite punctual, and I am just ready," said Chester, pushing back his chair, getting up, and going around to his wife's side of the table. "I will now take away the slanderer of your bright, talented, industrious young man," he remarked in sportive tone. "You shall be relieved of his presence until perhaps five o'clock this afternoon."

Before he had finished, Lucilla was standing by his side, her hand in his.

"Oh, dear! I wish you didn't have to go," she sighed. "We have been together all the time for weeks past, and now I hardly know how I can do without you."

"Suppose you come along then. There is plenty of room in the carriage and in the office, and I could find you something to read or some work on the typewriter, if you prefer that."

"Any time that I am needed there, I shall be ready to go," she returned with a merry look and tone, "but today I have matters to attend to about the house. Perhaps father and Mamma Vi may want some little assistance from me in their preparations for tonight, as well."

"Yes, I daresay. What a round of parties we are likely to have to go through as part of the penalty for venturing into the state of matrimony."

"Yes," laughed Lucilla. "I hope you think it pays."

"Most assuredly. But now good-bye, dearest, for some hours, when we shall have the pleasure of meeting to atone to us for the present pain of parting." Lucilla followed him to the veranda, where they exchanged a parting caress and watched as he entered the carriage. It drove swiftly through the grounds and out onto the highway. Her eyes were still following it when a pleasant manly voice near at hand said, "Good morning, Mrs. Dinsmore."

She turned quickly and sprang down the steps to meet the speaker.

"Father, dear father!" she cried, springing into his outstretched arms and putting hers about his neck. "Oh, how glad I am to see you! How good of you to come! Chester has just finished eating his breakfast and gone off to his business, and I haven't quite finished my meal. Won't you come in and eat with me?"

"Ah, that would hardly do, daughter," was the smiling reply. "You know I am expected to take that meal with wife and children at Woodburn. But I will go in with you, and we will have a chat while you finish your breakfast."

"You can take a cup of coffee and a little fruit. Can't you, father?"

"Yes, thank you, daughter. That would hardly interfere with the Woodburn breakfast. And shall we not take a little stroll about your grounds when we leave the breakfast room?"

"I should greatly enjoy doing so along with my dear father," she answered with a smiling look up into his face, as they took their places at the inviting-looking table. She poured his coffee, and they ate and chatted pleasantly all the while about family matters and the entertainment to be given at Woodburn that evening.

"How are Max and Eva this morning?" the Captain asked at length.

"I don't know whether they are up yet or not," replied Lucilla. "You know, papa, they had not the same occasion for early rising that Chester and I had."

"True enough, and Max is fully entitled to take his ease for the present. Don't you think so?"

"Yes, indeed, papa. I am glad the dear fellow is having a good holiday after all he has gone through. Oh, I wish he had chosen some business that would allow him to stay at home with us!"

"That would be more pleasant for us, but our country must have a navy and finely trained officers to command it."

"Yes, sir, and so it is well that some men fancy that kind of life and employment."

"And no doubt Max inherits the taste for a seafaring life from me and my forebears."

"Father," said Lulu, "you will let me be your amanuensis again. Will you not?"

"Thank you for your willingness to serve me in that, daughter," the Captain returned pleasantly. "But you will find quite enough to do here in your own house, and both your Mamma Vi and your sister Gracie have taken up your work in that line—sometimes one and sometimes the other following my dictation upon the typewriter."

"Oh, I am glad that they can and will, for your sake, father, but I hope I shall be permitted to do a little of my old work for you once in a while."

"That is altogether likely," he said. "But now, as we have finished eating and drinking, shall we not take our stroll about the grounds?"

They did so, chatting pleasantly as was their wont. Then returning to the veranda, they found Max and Evelyn there.

Morning greetings were exchanged. Evelyn stated that their breakfast was just ready and invited the Captain to come in and share it. But he declined, giving the same reason as before to Lucilla's invitation.

"I am going home now to breakfast with wife and children," he said, "and I hope you older ones of my flock will join us a little later."

"We will all be glad to do that, father," said Max. "At least I can speak for myself and think I can for these daughters of yours. Woodburn is to me a dear old home where some of the happiest hours of my life have been spent."

"And you can't love it much better than Lu and I do," added Evelyn.

"No, Max certainly can't love it any better," assented Lucilla. "Lovely as is this Sunnyside of ours, its chief attraction to me is its near neighborhood to Woodburn—the home where I have passed such happy years under my father's loving care." The bright, dark eyes she lifted to his face as she spoke were full of obvious daughterly love and reverence.

"I am very glad you can look back upon them as happy years, daughter," he said, his eyes shining with pleasure and parental affection, "and that Max is with you in that. I am glad, too, that you all appreciate this new home that I have taken so much pleasure in preparing for you."

"We'd be the basest of ingrates, if we didn't, father dear!" exclaimed Lucilla. "I for one, feel that you have done and are doing far more for me than I deserve."

"Which is nothing new for our father," remarked Max with a smile and look into his father's face that spoke volumes of filial regard, respect, and devotion.

"And I am fortunate, indeed, in having children so dutiful, affectionate, and appreciative," returned the Captain feelingly.

He then took his leave and went to Woodburn, Lucilla accompanying him part of the way. She then returned to Sunnyside to give her orders for the day. That attended to, she joined Max and Eva upon the veranda.

"The carriage is coming, Lu," said Eva. "Are you ready for a drive? And have you decided where you wish to go?"

"Yes," was the reply, "I want to go over to Woodburn for a bit of a chat with Mamma Vi about the preparations for this evening, in which I suppose you and Max will join me. Then wouldn't you like to drive over to Fairview for a call upon Aunt Elsie?"

"Yes, indeed! I think she and uncle are entitled to the first call from me, much as I want to see all the near and dear ones."

"I perfectly agree with you in that, Eva," said Max. "They have filled the place of parents to you, and I for one," he added with a lover-like smile, "am grateful to them for it."

"As I am also to them with still more reason," added Evelyn.

A few moments later found them on their way to Woodburn. There was a glad welcome there followed by a few minutes' lively chat principally in regard to the coming event of the evening—the expected gathering of invited guests, relatives, neighbors, and friends to welcome the return of the newly-married couples from their bridal trip.

"Is there anything I can do to help with your preparations, Mamma Vi?" asked Lucilla.

"Thank you, Lu, but they are almost all made now, except what the servants will do," returned Violet. "And if they were not, it would hardly be the correct thing to let one of our brides be at the trouble of assisting with them."

"Both of them would be very glad to give their help, if it were desired or needed," said Evelyn. "We feel privileged to offer assistance, because it is our father's house," she concluded with a smiling, affectionate look at the captain.

"That is right, daughter," he said, both his tone and the expression of his countenance showing that he was pleased with her remark.

"Oh, Lu, I have been making some changes in the rooms that were yours but are mine now," said Gracie. "Papa has provided some new pieces of furniture both there and in our little sitting room, and I want to show them to you, Eva, and Max." She rose as she spoke, the others following her example.

"Are the rest of us invited, Gracie?" asked Violet in an amused tone.

"Oh, yes, indeed!" was the merry rejoinder. "Father and you, Elsie and Ned are company that is always acceptable to me wherever I go."

"And to all of us," added Lucilla.

"Most especially so to one who has often sighed in vain for it," said Max.

"Have you wanted us sometimes when you were far away on the sea, Brother Max?" asked Ned with a look of loving sympathy up into his brother's face.

"Yes, indeed, Ned, and I expect to do so again before very long."

They were passing through the hall and up the stairway as they talked. "Oh, the dear, old rooms look lovely, lovely!" exclaimed Lucilla, as they passed into the little sitting room she had formerly shared with her sister Gracie. She glanced around it and through the open doors into the two bedrooms. "It almost makes me homesick to be living in them again."

"Well, daughter, you may come back to them whenever you choose," her father said with a look of mingled amusement and affection.

"Why, Lu, I thought you loved that pretty new home papa has taken such pains to make ready for you and Eva and Max and Chester," exclaimed Elsie.

"Yes, so I do, but this old home has the added charm of being papa's also."

"Yes, but the other is so near that you can see him every day, and oftener, if you choose."

"And talk to him at any moment through the telephone, if she prefers that to coming over here," said the captain.

"Oh, yes! How nice it is that our houses are all connected by telephone," exclaimed Evelyn. "Father, if I may, I think I'll go to yours and speak to Aunt Elsie now."

"Certainly, daughter," he returned, promptly leading the way.

"I do so like that name from you, father dear," she said softly and smiling up into his face as they reached the instrument.

"And I am glad my boy Max has given me the right," he returned, bending down to kiss the soft cheek and smooth her shining hair.

"Shall I ring and call for you?" he asked.

"If you please."

It was Mrs. Leland who answered.

"Hello, what is it?"

"It is I, Aunt Elsie," returned Evelyn. "I just called to find out if you were in. We had planned to come over directly to make a call upon you."

"I think I shall be by the time you can get here," was the reply in a tone of amusement. "But please don't delay, as we were about to start for Sunnyside in a few minutes."

"Oh, were you! Then we'll drive over at once and accompany you on the trip."

"Thank you. That will be most pleasant."

Eva stepped aside, and Lucilla took her place.

"Yes, Aunt Elsie, you will be a most welcome visitor in both divisions of Sunnyside. Please don't neglect mine."

"I certainly do not intend to," was the cheery response. "For your half of the dwelling is quite as well worth seeing as the other, and its two occupants seem very near and dear."

"Thank you, Aunt Elsie. Good-bye now until we arrive at Fairview."

"We had better start for that place presently," said Max. "We can view the beauties of this any day. Won't you go with us, Gracie? There is a vacant seat in the carriage."

"Yes, do. We'd be glad to have you," urged both Eva and Lucilla. The latter added, "You have hardly yet taken a look at our new homes with us in them."

"Yes, go, daughter. I think you will enjoy it," her father said in reply to a questioning glance from the beautiful eyes directed to him.

"Thank you all three," she said. "I will go if I may have ten minutes in which to get ready."

"Fifteen, if necessary," replied Max in sportive tone. "Even that great loss of time will be well paid for by the pleasure of your good company."

"A well-turned compliment, brother mine," returned Gracie, as she tripped away in search of hat and wrap, for the air was cool in driving.

"Why shouldn't Elsie go, too? There is plenty of room for her, and Ned can ride alongside on his pony, which I see is down yonder already saddled and bridled," said Max, putting an arm around his little sister, as she stood by his side, and looking smilingly at her, then at Ned. "Can't they go, father and Mamma Vi?"

Both parents gave a ready consent. The children were delighted with the invitation, and presently the party set out on their way to Fairview.

It was a short and pleasant drive, and they were greeted with a joyous welcome on their arrival at Evelyn's old home. Mr. and Mrs. Leland and their four children met them on the veranda with smiles, pleasant words, and caresses for Gracie, Eva, Lucilla, and Elsie. Then they were taken within and to the dining room, where a delicate and appetizing lunch was awaiting them.

"It is a little early for lunch," said Mrs. Leland, "but we knew you would be wanting to get back to Sunnyside soon in order not to miss the numerous calls about to be made you by friends and connections who are all anxious to see the pretty new home and its loved occupants."

"We will be glad to see them, Aunt Elsie," said Evelyn, "and to show our lovely home. I can assure you that no one can be more welcome there than you and uncle and these dear cousins of mine."

"Please understand that Eva has expressed my sentiments as fully as her own," added Lucilla in a sprightly tone.

"Mine also," said Max.

"But don't any one of you feel that this meal is to be taken in haste," said Mr. Leland, hospitably. "That is very bad for digestion, and we may take plenty of time, even at the risk of having some of your callers get to Sunnyside ahead of us."

His advice was taken and much pleasant chat indulged in while they ate.

"You and uncle, of course, expect to be at Woodburn tonight, Aunt Elsie?" said Evelyn.

"Oh, yes, and we expect to have you all here tomorrow night. There is to be quite a round of parties—as doubtless you know—to celebrate the great event of your and Lu's entrance into the bonds of matrimony. There will be none Saturday night, but the round will begin again Monday evening by a party at Ion given by mamma, Edward, and Zoe. Tuesday evening we are all to go to the Oaks, then after that to the Laurels, Roselands, Beechwood, Pinegrove, Ashlands, and others."

"Please don't forget Aunt Rosie's party at Riverside, too, mamma," prompted Allie, her nine-year-old daughter.

"No," returned her mother, "that would be quite too bad, for there is no one more ready to do honor to these dear friends of ours—especially now when they have just begun married life."

"Ah, Aunt Elsie, that sounds as though you considered it something to one's credit to have left a life of single blessedness for one in the married state," laughed Lucilla.

"A state I have found so pleasant that I think no one deserves any credit for entering it," was Mrs. Leland's smiling rejoinder.

"And I have noticed," said Max, "that as a rule those who have tried it once are very ready to try it again—widows and widowers seem in more haste to marry than bachelors and maids."

"'Marry in haste and repent at leisure,'" quoted Gracie laughingly. "Father takes care that his children don't do the first, perhaps to secure them from the second."

"And we all have great confidence in our father's wisdom, as well as his strong affection for us, his children," remarked Max.

A sentiment which the others—his wife and sisters—promptly and cordially endorsed.

CHAPTER SECOND

IMMEDIATELY UPON LEAVING the table, they all — entertainers and entertained — set out on the short drive to Sunnyside, where, upon arriving, they found their relatives and friends from Beechwood and the Oaks waiting to offer their congratulations and wish them happiness and prosperity in their married life.

Being all acquaintances and friends of so long standing, they were shown over the whole house by the happy owners, and some very cordial congratulations were freely bestowed.

"In view of the comforts, conveniences, and beauties of the establishment, I should like to see Chester and offer my congratulations on his success in winning a lovely wife and having so delightful a home to share with her," remarked Mrs. Horace Dinsmore, as she was about to leave. "But I can't stay any longer if I am to make due preparation for attending the party at Woodburn tonight," she added.

"And you wouldn't miss that for anything. Would you?" laughed Mrs. Hugh Lilburn. "I am sure I wouldn't."

"No, for I daresay we will have a delightful time. I know no better entertainers than the captain and Vi."

"Nor do I," said Mrs. Leland, "and this being such a special occasion, they will doubtless do their best."

"I think they will, and I hope no invited quest will stay away or be disappointed," said Gracie with a merry look and smile.

"No danger of either calamity, Gracie," said Mrs. Dinsmore. "Ah, there is our carriage at the door," and with a hasty good-bye and a cordial invitation to all present to make frequent visits at the Oaks, she and her husband and daughter departed.

The Beechwood friends lingered a little longer, as did those from Fairview and Woodburn. But at length, Gracie said she thought it time to go home, for, of course, there were some matters she ought to attend to in preparation for the evening.

"Shall I send you in the carriage?" asked Lucilla sweetly.

"Oh, no, thank you, sister dear. The short walk will be good for me," returned Gracie merrily, "for Elsie, too, I think, and for Ned. Though he, I suppose, will prefer to ride his pony."

"Yes, of course, I will," said Ned. "He needs to be taken home, anyway."

They made their adieus and moved out on the shady veranda.

A servant brought the pony up, and Ned was about to mount when the little steed remarked, "I think a young gentleman might feel ashamed to ride while his lady sisters must go afoot."

"You do!" exclaimed Ned, drawing back with look of mingled surprise and chagrin. "Well, they said they wanted to walk—preferred it to riding, and besides they couldn't both ride on your back at once."

"Two do ride the same horse at the same time sometimes," seemed to come very distinctly from the pony's lips.

"Who is making you talk, I wonder?" cried Ned, turning to look about him. "Oh, Brother Max, it was you. Wasn't it?" as he caught sight of his brother and sisters standing near.

"What was?" asked Max quietly.

"The person making the pony talk. I almost thought for a minute it really was the pony. Though, of course, ponies can't talk, and I didn't mean to be selfish. Gracie, won't you ride him home? Elsie and I can walk just as well as not."

"Yes, of course, we can. It's a very short and very pleasant walk," returned Elsie with prompt cheerfulness. "So, Gracie dear, you ride the pony home."

"Thank you both," said Gracie, "but I really prefer to walk, as I have had very little outdoor exercise today."

"There, you silly pony, see what a mistake you made!" cried Ned gleefully, as he expertly mounted his steed.

"Well, little master, didn't you make a mistake, too?" the pony seemed to ask.

"Oh, Brother Max, I know it's you, so only good fun," laughed Ned. "Good-bye all. I'll get home first and tell papa and mamma you are coming, Gracie and Elsie."

With the last words, he galloped down the avenue, leaving Max and his sisters standing on the veranda looking after him.

"Doesn't he ride well?" exclaimed Gracie in a tone that spoke much sisterly pride and affection. The others gave a hearty assent.

Max added, "He is a dear, bright, little chap. I am decidedly proud of my only brother."

"As I am of my little one, but I am still more so of my older one," said Lucilla. "But I must go back to my remaining guests. Good-bye, my two dear sisters. I shall expect and hope to see you both over here every day."

"It is very likely you will see us here at least that often," laughed Gracie, "and we will expect an honest return of each and every visit."

"We'll get it, too," cried Elsie. "Lu could never stay away a whole day from papa."

"It would certainly take a very, very strong compulsion to make me do so," said Lucilla. "Good-bye again. I hope to see you both in my old home a few hours hence and again tomorrow."

With that, she returned to her guests in the house while her two younger sisters hastened away in the direction of Woodburn.

"It will soon be time to send the carriage for Chester," commented Max, accompanying her. "Suppose I give the order now."

"Yes, please do," she replied. "I'd like to have him here as soon as possible, and if he should not be quite ready, Jack and the carriage can be kept waiting for him."

"Certainly. I'll go and give the order and then rejoin you and our guests in the drawing room."

As Max stepped out upon the veranda again, two carriages came driving up the avenue—one bringing Mr. and Mrs. Lacey from the Laurels, the other Mr. and Mrs. Croly from Riverside.

"Oh, Max, how glad I am to see you again!" exclaimed Rosie, as he assisted her to alight. "It seems an age since you went away, and you have been exposed to such perils! I hope I shall have a chance to hear the story of your experiences in that fight at Manila. Such a chance as I couldn't get at any of the parties."

"Thank you, I hope we will have time and opportunity for a number of talks," he replied, releasing the hand she had put into his and turning to greet Mrs. Lacey, whom he addressed as Aunt Rose and whose greeting was quite as cordial as her niece's had been.

"You have the Fairview and Beechwood folks here now I see," remarked Mrs. Croly, glancing toward their waiting vehicles.

"Yes, please walk in and let us have you all together," returned Max. "We will make a small party in anticipation of the larger one to be held at Woodburn some hours hence."

"Yes," assented Rosie, "we are all relatives and friends, and I for one can never see too much of

Elsie or Cousin Ronald—to speak of only one of each family."

Hearty greetings were exchanged all around, a short time spent in cheerful chat, then one set of visitors after another took their departure until at length Max, Evelyn, and Lucilla were left alone, though looking almost momentarily for Chester's homecoming.

"It has probably been a hard day with him. I fear he will be too weary for much enjoyment tonight," sighed Lucilla.

"I hope not," said Max. "The meeting with so many relatives and friends will probably be restful. Ah, there's the carriage now, just coming up the driveway."

It brought Chester, and he showed himself to be in excellent spirits, though somewhat weary with the labors of the day. He reported that all seemed to be going right with the business at hand, and he had little doubt that he should gain his hoped-for reward. His audience of three listened with keen interest to all he had to say. When he had finished, Eva rose, saying, "I must go now and attend to housekeeping matters so that Max and I may be ready in good season for our Woodburn festivities."

"Stay, Eva," said Lucilla, "I have ordered an early light tea for the four of us. We won't want a hearty meal to spoil our appetites for the refreshments to be served at Woodburn."

"No, certainly not. It is kind of you to provide for us as well as for yourselves," said Evelyn.

Max added, "It is, indeed, sister mine."

"Well, really," laughed Lucilla, "it was for my own pleasure quite as much as for yours." And tears came into the eyes gazing with sisterly affection into those of Max. "I want to entertain you while I can," she added. "For there is no knowing when Uncle Sam may be ordering you quite out of reach."

"Oh, don't let us talk of that!" exclaimed Eva. "Let us banish it from all of our thoughts for the present."

"That is good advice," said Max, his voice a trifle husky. "It's what I'm trying to do for the present. However much a man may love the service, a little wife such as mine must be far nearer and dearer."

"Yes," said Chester. "If you had only chosen the law, we might now be partners in my office, as well as in this house."

"Perhaps I might ruin the business by my stupidity," returned Max with playful a look and tone.

"Hark! There's the tea bell," said Lucilla. "I invite you all out to the dining room."

After a pleasant social half-hour spent at the tea table, each couple retired to their own apartments to dress for the planned evening of entertainment at Woodburn.

"This is one of the occasions for the wearing of your lovely wedding gown. Is it not?" Max inquired of Evelyn, as they moved into her dressing room.

"Yes," she said lightly. "You will not mind seeing me in it for the second time. Will you?"

"I shall be very glad to. It is both beautiful and becoming," he returned with a fond look and smile. "Ah, my Eva, I think no one ever had a sweeter bride than mine," he added, passing his arm about her and drawing her into a close embrace.

"They say love is blind, and it must be that which makes me look so lovely in your eyes. My features are by no means so good and regular as those of some others—your sisters Lu and Gracie, for instance," returned Evelyn with a pleased little laugh.

"Those two sisters of mine are both very beautiful in my eyes, but there is something—to me—still sweeter in this dear face," he answered to that, giving her a fond and loving caress as he spoke.

"And your love is so sweet to me, I am so glad to belong to you," she returned low and feelingly, laying her head on his chest while glad tears shone in her eyes. "I have only one cause for grief left," she went on presently, "that we cannot live together all the time, as Lu and Chester may. Yet, in spite of that, I would not change with her or anybody else."

"I hope not, darling," he said laughingly. "Nor would I any more than you. I think we were made for each other."

"So do I, and when compelled to part for a season, we will console ourselves by looking forward to the joy of the reunion."

"So we will, dear one, and in the meantime, we will have the pleasure of correspondence."

"Yes, indeed! A letter from my husband will be a great treasure and delight to me."

"Not more than will be one from my wife to me," he returned, giving her a gleeful caress.

In the meantime, Chester and his Lucilla were similarly engaged. Chester was very proud and fond of his bride and anxious to show her to neighbors and friends in her wedding dress. So, he expressed his satisfaction when he saw it laid out in readiness for the occasion.

"I am glad it pleases you," said Lucilla, "and I own to liking it myself. Eva is going to wear hers, too. It will seem something like a reception of our wedding day."

"Which makes it very suitable for your father's house. It was a disappointment to him, I know, not to have his children married in his own house."

"Yes, I suppose so, but dear father is so unselfish that he preferred to let us have our own way, especially on Eva's account."

"I know it, and I mean to try to copy his fine example in that — seeking to please others rather than myself."

"As I do. I should so much like to resemble him in character and conduct as much as some people tell me I do in both my features and facial expressions."

"Yes, you are very like him in both," Chester said with an affectionate and admiring look and smile, "in character and conduct also, if your admiring husband be any judge."

The Sunnyside couples were the first of the guests to reach Woodburn—though, in fact, they hardly considered themselves guests or were deemed such by the family there. It was but going home to their father's house, where they had an hour of keen enjoyment before the other relatives and guests began to arrive.

Everything went smoothly. The company was made up of congenial spirits, and the entertainment was fine and evidently enjoyed. When they bade goodnight and scattered to their homes, it was with the expectation of meeting again the next evening at Fairview. The Dinsmores of the Oaks had planned to give the second entertainment, but Mr. and Mrs. Leland claimed it as their right, because of their near relationship to Evelyn and the fact that Fairview had been her home for so many years.

They were now nearing the end of the week. This was Thursday, and the Fairview party would be held on Friday evening. Saturday, all preferred to spend quietly in their own homes or with their nearest and dearest, and that plan was carried out. The Fairview party passed off as successfully as the Woodburn one, and Saturday and Sunday brought a rest from festivities that was welcomed to all.

✿✿✿✿✿✿✿✿

CHAPTER THIRD

LUCILLA COULD NEVER stay long away from her old home in her father's house. She was there every day and often two or three times a day.

"Father," she said on that first Saturday after taking possession of the new home, "mayn't we Sunnyside folks come over here and join your Bible class tomorrow evening?"

"My dear child, it is just what I would have you do," he returned with a gratified and loving smile. "Don't forget that Woodburn is still your home—one of your homes at least—and that you are always welcome and more than welcome to join us when you will. You are my own daughter as truly as ever you were."

"And just as glad to be as ever I was," she exclaimed with a bright, loving look and smile, "to do your bidding at all times, father dear," she added.

"Provided it does not interfere with Chester's," Max, who happened to be present, suggested a little mischievously.

"Hardly any danger of that, I think," remarked his father with a slightly amused look. "Chester is a reasonable fellow, and I have no intention of interfering with his rights."

"And he thinks almost as highly of my father's wisdom as I do," said Lucilla.

"But not more than Max and I do," said Evelyn, giving the captain a very filial and admiring look. "You will take us in as members of your class, too. Won't you, father?"

"It is just what I desire to do," was the pleased reply. "Max has always been a member when at home, and you, you know, are now his better half."

Eva shook her head and with a merry, laughing look at Max, said, "Not just that, father. I should say the smaller partner in the firm."

"That will do, too," smiled the captain. "Since the most costly goods are apt to be done up in the smallest packages."

"Ah, Eva, my dear, you are answered," laughed Max.

"What is the subject of tomorrow's lesson, captain?" asked Mrs. Elsie Travilla, sitting near.

"I have not decided that question yet, mother, and I should be glad of a suggestion from you," he replied in a kindly, respectful tone.

"I have been thinking a good deal lately of the signs of the times," she said, "and whether they do not show that we are nearing the end times. That might perhaps be a profitable and interesting question to take up and endeavor to solve."

"No doubt it would," he replied, "and I hope you will come prepared to give us some good information as to what the Scriptures say on the subject and what are the views of Biblical scholars who have been giving it particular attention."

"I will do what I can in that line, and I hope you, captain, and others will come prepared to take part in considering the subject."

"Certainly a most interesting one," said Violet.

"And one which must lead to great searching of the Scriptures as the only infallible source of information," added the captain.

"Yes," said Grandma Elsie, "they are the only authority on that subject. And how thankful we should be that we have them."

Sabbath afternoon proved bright and clear, and it brought to Woodburn quite a gathering of the relatives and friends. All loved the Bible studies they had for years taken together.

Mr. Lilburn, as the eldest, was persuaded to take the lead.

"I understand," he said, "that today we are to take up the question whether the second coming of our Lord Jesus Christ may, or may not, be near. The Scriptures are our sole authority, and you are all invited to bring forward anything from them that may seem to you to have a bearing on the subject." Turning to Mrs. Travilla, "Cousin Elsie," he said, "you are, probably, the one among us the most thoroughly prepared to do so. Please, let us hear from you."

"I doubt if I am better prepared than some of the rest of you," she replied, "but I have been very much interested in the subject, particularly of late. I have searched the Bible for texts bearing upon it, some of which I will read. Here in the first chapter of Acts, we read that the disciples asked, "'Lord, wilt thou at this time restore again the kingdom Israel?" And He said to them, "It is not for you to know the times or the seasons, which the Father hath put in His own power. But ye shall receive power, after that the Holy Ghost is come upon you: and ye shall be witnesses unto Me both in Jerusalem and in all Judea, and in Samaria, and unto the uttermost part of the earth." And when He had spoken these things, while they beheld, He was taken up; and a cloud received Him out of their sight. And while they looked steadfastly toward heaven as He went up, behold, two men stood by them in white apparel; which also said, "Ye men of Galilee, why stand ye gazing up into Heaven? This same Jesus which is taken up from you into Heaven, shall so come in like manner as ye have seen Him go into Heaven."' And," continued Grandma Elsie, "the apostle John gives us the same promise here in the first chapter of Revelation," turning to the passage as she spoke, reading it aloud, "'Behold, He cometh with clouds; and every eye shall see Him.'"

"I have heard the idea advanced that death is the coming of Christ to the dying one," remarked Chester in a tone of inquiry.

"But we are told," said Mrs. Travilla, "that 'as the lightning cometh out of the east, and shineth even unto the west; so shall also the coming of the Son of Man be.' That description certainly could not apply to the death hour of any Christian nor to the conversion of any sinner."

"And His second coming is spoken of in the same way in a number of places in the different gospels," said Evelyn. "Here in Luke, we have Christ's own words, 'Whosoever shall be ashamed of Me and of My words, of him shall the Son of Man be ashamed, when He shall come in His glory, and in His Father's, and of the holy angels.' And again in Matthew 16:27, 'For the Son of Man shall come in the glory of His Father with His angels; and then He shall reward every man according to his works.'"

"The disciples wanted to know when that second coming would be," remarked Violet. "Here in Matthew 24:3, we are told, 'And as He sat upon the Mount of Olives, the disciples came unto Him privately, saying, "Tell us, when shall these things be? And what shall be the sign of Thy coming, and of the end of the world?" And Jesus answered and said unto them, "Take heed that no man deceive you."'

"I shall not read the whole chapter, for I know it is familiar to you all, but in the twenty-seventh verse, as mamma already quoted, He says, 'For as the lightning cometh out of the east, and shineth even unto the west; so shall also the coming of the Son of Man be. For wheresoever the carcass is, there will the eagles be gathered together. Immediately after the tribulation of those days shall the sun be darkened, and the moon shall not give her light, and the stars shall fall from Heaven, and the powers of the Heavens shall be shaken: and then shall appear the sign of the Son of Man in Heaven: and then shall all the tribes of the earth mourn, and they shall see the Son of Man coming in the clouds of Heaven with power and great glory. And He shall send His angels with a great sound of a trumpet, and they shall gather together His elect from the four winds, from one end of Heaven to the other.'"

"Many persons," returned Grandma Elsie, "tell us it is not worthwhile to consider at all the question of the time when Christ will come again. They often quote the text, 'But of that day and hour knoweth no man, no, not the angels in Heaven, but my Father only.' But again and again our Saviour repeated His warning, 'Watch, therefore; for ye know not what hour your Lord doth come . . . Therefore be ye also ready: for in such an hour as ye think not the Son of Man cometh.'"

"I do not quite understand this," said Gracie. "Luke says, here in the twenty-first chapter and the twentieth verse, quoting the words of the Master: 'And when ye shall see Jerusalem compassed with armies, then know that the desolation thereof is nigh. Then let them which are in Judea flee to the mountains; and let them which are in the midst of it depart out.' How could they depart out of the city while it was compassed with armies?"

"There is a satisfactory explanation," replied her father. "In the twelfth year of Nero, Cestius Gallus, the president of Syria, came against Jerusalem with a powerful army. Josephus says of him: 'He might have assaulted and taken the city, and thereby put an end to the war. Not without any just reason, and contrary to the expectation of all, he raised the siege and departed.' The historians, Epiphanius and Eusebius, tell us that immediately after the departure of the armies of Cestius Gallus and while Vespasian was approaching with his army all who believed in Christ left Jerusalem and fled to Pella and other places beyond the river Jordan."

"Every one of them, papa?" asked Ned.

"Yes, my son. Dr. Adam Clarke says: 'It is very remarkable that not a single Christian perished in the destruction of Jerusalem, though there were many there when Cestius Gallus invested the city.'"

"Papa," asked Elsie, "don't you think God put it in the heart of that Cestius Gallus to go away with his troops before Vespassian got there—so that all of the Christians had a good opportunity to escape?"

"I certainly do, daughter," was the Captain's emphatic reply.

"Had not the earlier prophets foretold the destruction of Jerusalem?" asked Lucilla.

"Yes," said Mr. Lilburn, "even as early as Moses. Here in the twenty-eighth chapter of Deuteronomy, he says, 'The Lord shall bring a nation against thee from far, from the end of the earth, as swift as the eagle flieth; a nation whose tongue thou shalt not understand.'"

"The Romans?" Elsie said, inquiringly.

"Yes. Their ensign was an eagle and their language the Latin, which the Jews did not understand. The prophecy of Moses continues. In the fifty-second verse, he says, 'And he shall besiege thee in all thy gates, until thy high and fenced walls come down, wherein thou trustedst, throughout thy land: and he shall besiege thee in all thy gates throughout all thy land, which the Lord thy God hath given thee. And thou shalt eat the fruit of thine own body, the flesh of thy sons and of thy daughters, which the Lord thy God hath given thee, in the siege and in the straitness wherein thine enemies shall distress thee.'"

"Oh, how dreadful!" exclaimed Elsie. "And did all that happen at the siege of Jerusalem?"

"Yes. It lasted so long that famine was added to all the other sufferings of the besieged. So dreadful was it that mothers would snatch food from their children in their distress, and many houses were found full of women and children who had died of starvation. Josephus tells of human flesh being eaten—particularly of a lady of rank who killed, roasted, and ate her own son. And so the prophecy of Moses was fulfilled."

"Oh, how dreadful, how very, very dreadful!" sighed little Elsie.

"Yes," said Mr. Lilburn, "it was the fulfillment of our Savior's prophecy as He beheld Jerusalem and wept over it, saying, 'If thou hadst known, even thou, at least in this thy day, the things which belong unto thy peace! But now they are hid from thine eyes. For the days shall come upon thee, that thine enemies shall cast a trench about thee, and compass thee round, and keep thee in on every side, and shall lay thee even with the ground, and thy children within thee; and they shall not leave in thee one stone upon another; because thou knewest not the time of thy visitation.' That is told us in the nineteenth chapter of Luke. In the twenty-first, we read, 'And they shall fall by the edge of the sword, and shall be led away captive into all nations: and Jerusalem shall be trodden down of the Gentiles, until the times of the Gentiles be fulfilled.'"

"Have those times been fulfilled yet?" asked Ned quietly.

"No, not yet," replied Mr. Lilburn. "The Turks still have possession of Jerusalem, though the Jews have begun to return to Palestine, and the Turkish power grows weaker. But the time of the Gentiles will not be fulfilled until the work of the Gospel is finished."

"And when will that be, Cousin Ronald?" asked Ned.

"I cannot say exactly," answered the elder gentleman, "but the trend of events does seem to show that we are nearing that time—such a feeling of unrest all over the world. This is a such a land of plenty, and but for the grasping selfishness of some, none need lack for abundance of the necessaries of life."

"I wish nobody did lack for plenty to eat and drink and wear," said little Elsie. "I want to do all I can to help those who haven't enough."

"I hope you will, daughter," the Captain said in a tone of pleased approval. "Now, the important thing for us to consider is what is our duty in view of the nearness of Christ's second coming."

"He has told us again and again to watch and be ready," said Grandma Elsie. "We are not to be idle, but we are to work while it is called today, to occupy till He comes, to be not slothful in business, fervent in spirit, serving the Lord."

Chapter Fourth

For the next week or two, family parties for the honor and entertainment of the newly-married ones were frequent. Life seemed to them bright and joyous, except when they remembered that Max would probably soon be ordered away, perhaps to some distant quarter of the globe. It was an unwelcome anticipation not to the two newlyweds only, but to Captain Raymond and the others at Woodburn and in a slighter degree to all the connection. But orders had not come yet, and they still hoped they might be delayed for weeks, giving opportunity for many quiet home pleasures. Yet, there were drawbacks to even those in the fact that several of the near connection were ailing from colds caught during their round of festivities — Grandma Elsie and Chester Dinsmore being of those most seriously affected. Chester was confined to the house for several days under the doctor's care, and it was against medical advice that he then returned to his labors at his office. Lucilla was troubled and anxious, and, as usual, went to her father for sympathy and advice. They had a chat together in the library at Woodburn.

"I feel for you, daughter," Captain Raymond said, "but keep up your courage. 'All is not lost that is in danger.' I have been thinking that a southerly trip in the yacht might prove of benefit to both Grandma Elsie and Chester and quite as agreeable to the members of our family and other friends for whom we could find room."

"Oh, father, that would be delightful!" she exclaimed, her eyes sparkling with pleasure. "And I hope you will persuade Harold to make one of the company for Gracie's sake and so that we will not be without a physician."

"Yes, that is a part of my plan, and I have little doubt of its acceptance. Gracie's companionship is certainly a very great attraction to my young brother-in-law."

"'Speak of angels and you will hear the flutter of wings,'" laughed Lucilla, as at that moment Harold appeared in the doorway.

"Am I the angel, and may I fly in?" he asked, joining in the laugh.

"Certainly, you are just in the nick of time to advise us in a matter of importance which we are discussing," replied the Captain, inviting him by a gesture to an easy chair near at hand, repeating to him the substance of what he had been saying to Lucilla, and finishing with a request for his opinion in regard to the plan.

"I like it extremely," Harold said. "I think that nothing could be better for either my mother or Chester, and the sooner we make ready and start the better for both, if they will be persuaded to go, of which I have little doubt."

"I am somewhat afraid Chester may refuse for business reasons," sighed Lucilla.

"I think we can persuade him of the folly of that," said her father. "It would be far wiser and better to give up business for a time for the gaining of health than to so wreck that by overtaxing strength of body and mind as to shorten his days or make himself an invalid for life."

"It certainly would," said Harold, "and I hope that among us we can convince him that duty, as well as pleasure, calls him to make one of the party."

"Duty to his wife as well as to himself," said Lucilla in a lively tone, "for I should neither willingly go without him or stay behind with him."

"Where are Vi, Gracie, and the children?" asked Harold. "I have not seen or heard anything of them since I came in."

"Max and Eva have taken them driving in our fine new carriage—father's wedding gift," replied Lucilla with a smiling glance into her father's eyes. "That is, all but Ned who rides his pony alongside."

"Ah, and here they come now!" exclaimed Harold, glancing from the window. "The carriage has just turned in at the gates."

With that, the three arose and hastened out to the veranda to greet and assist them to alight. But the moment the carriage drew up before the entrance, the door was thrown open. Max, then Chester, sprang out and turned to hand out the ladies—Grandma Elsie, Eva, Violet, Gracie, and Elsie, while at the very same time Ned was dismounting his pony.

Warm greetings were exchanged, and as the weather was now too cool for comfortable sitting upon the veranda, the Captain led the way to the library—a favorite resort with them all.

"Your call is an agreeable surprise, mother," he said to Grandma Elsie, as he drew forward an easy chair for her. "Harold had just been telling us that you were almost ill with a cold."

"I have a rather bad one, but I thought a drive through the bracing air and in such pleasant company might prove beneficial rather than otherwise," she answered in cheery tones. "And I knew Harold was here and could take me home in his conveyance."

"Certainly, mother, and I will be very glad of your good company," said Harold.

At the same time, Violet exclaimed, "But why go at all tonight, mother? Why not stay here tonight with us?"

"Thank you, daughter," was the smiling reply. "That would be pleasant, but there are some things to be attended to at home."

"And not being well, she would better have her doctor close at hand," remarked Harold in playful tones. "Mother, we have been contriving a plan to help you and Chester to get the better of your illness."

"Ah, what is that?" she asked.

Harold, turning at once to the captain, said, "Let mother hear it from you, Brother Levis, if you please."

"We are thinking of taking a southward trip in the *Dolphin*, mother, to visit the Bermudas, other islands of the West Indies, and the coast of Brazil."

"Why, that would be a lovely trip!" she exclaimed. "Many thanks to you, captain, for including me among your invited guests."

"Many thanks to you, mother, if you consent to be one of our party," he returned, looking greatly pleased to find her so ready to approve of and share their plans.

Eager, excited remarks and queries now followed in rapid succession from the others present. "When would the start be made? Who besides Grandma Elsie and the captain were to compose the party?"

"All who are here now are each invited and expected to go—some others of our friends also," replied the captain. "I hope no one will refuse."

"Many warm thanks, captain," said Chester. "I should be delighted to go, but I fear business will prevent."

"As your physician, Ches, I strongly advise you not to let it," said Harold. "A good rest now in a warm climate may restore you to vigorous health. If you stay at home and stick to business, you are likely to either cut your life short or make yourself a confirmed invalid for the rest of it."

"Do you really think so, cousin doctor?" was Chester's rejoinder in a troubled voice.

"I do most emphatically," returned Harold. "You may be very thankful, cousin, that this good opportunity offers."

"I am," said Chester. Turning to the captain, he said, "Thank you very much, sir, for the invitation, which I accept, if my wife will go with me."

"You needn't doubt that," laughed Lucilla. "There is nothing I like better than a trip on my father's yacht with him and all of my dear ones about me."

"And it's just the same with all the rest of us," said Gracie.

"How is it with Max and Eva?" asked the captain.

"I know of nothing more enjoyable than a trip—a trip on the *Dolphin* taken in the company of one's dear ones," replied Evelyn with a loving look into the eyes of her young husband.

"Just my opinion," he said with a smile. "The only question with me is will Uncle Sam allow me a sufficiently long leave of absence."

"Your leave of absence has nearly expired?" his father said inquiringly.

"Yes, sir. So nearly that I should hardly feel surprised to receive orders any day."

"Well, I hope, instead, you may get another leave, allowing you time to make one of our party on this trip."

"It would be a great pleasure to me, sir," said Max. "But I have had so long a one already that I can hardly hope for another one very soon."

"Oh, Max!" exclaimed Gracie. "Do write at once asking to have it extended. It would double our pleasure to have you along."

"Yes, Max, do," said Lucilla. "I can hardly bear the thought of going without you."

Evelyn, sitting close at his side, looked her entreaties, and Violet said, "Yes, Max, do. It will certainly double our enjoyment to have both you and Eva along."

Then Chester, Grandma Elsie, Harold, and the children added their entreaties, expressing their desire for his company on the trip. Ned exclaimed, "Yes, Brother Max, do get leave to go along. We'll want you to make fun for us with your ventriloquism."

"Is that all you want me for, Neddie boy?" laughed Max. "If so, Cousin Ronald will answer your purpose quite as well, if not better."

"But two can make more fun than one, and I want you besides. I am really fond of you—the only brother I've got."

"Ah, that sounds better," said Max, "but I can't go without Uncle Sam's permission."

"Then please do ask him to give it."

"Yes, do, Max," said Gracie. "I really think he might give it, considering what good service you did him in Manila."

"It was not very much that I accomplished personally," returned Max modestly. "The two months' rest I have had is probably quite as much as I may be supposed to have earned, especially as it gave me the opportunity to secure my wife," he added with a very affectionate look down into Evelyn's eyes.

"I wish you might be able to go with us, Max, my son," said the captain. "Leaving ventriloquism entirely out of the account, I should be very glad to have your company. But the service, of course, has the first claim on you."

"So I think, sir. And as for the ventriloquism my little brother is so hungry for, Cousin Ronald can supply it should you take him as one of your passengers on the journey."

"And we will, if he and his wife can be persuaded to go," returned the captain heartily.

"Oh, good, papa!" cried Ned, clapping his hands in glee. "Then we'll have at least one ventriloquist: if we can't have two."

"And, after all, the ventriloquism was really all you wanted me for, eh?" said Max, assuming a tone and look of chagrin.

"Oh, no! No! Brother Max," cried Ned with a look of distress. "I didn't mean that! You know you're the only brother I have, and I'm really fond of you."

"As I am of you, little brother, and I have been ever since you were born," said Max, regarding the little fellow with an affectionate smile.

"Oh, Max, I wish you hadn't gone into the navy," sighed Lucilla.

"I don't," he returned, cheerfully. "Though I acknowledge that it is hard parting with home and dear ones."

"That is bad, as I know by experience," said their father, "but then we have the compensating joy of the many reunions."

"Yes, sir, and a great joy it is," responded Max. "How soon, father, do you think of starting on your southward trip?"

"Just as soon as all necessary arrangements can be made, which, I suppose, will not be more than a week from this, at farthest. I can have the yacht made ready in less time than that, and for the sake of our invalids, it would be well to go as promptly as possible."

"Couldn't you make good use of the telephone now to give your invitations, my dear?" queried Violet lightly.

"Why, yes. That is a wise suggestion. I will do so at once," he replied and hastily left the room, promising to return presently with the reply from Beechwood to which he would call first.

The invitation was accepted promptly and with evident pleasure, as the captain presently reported to the library.

"Now, mother, shall I give my invitation in the same way to our own friends?" he asked, turning to Grandma Elsie.

"Perhaps it would be as well to send it by Harold and me," she said, "as that will delay it very little. I can perhaps help them to perceive what a delightful trip it is likely to prove."

"And then, mamma, you can give us their view by the phone," said Violet.

"I or some one of the family will," she said. "And now, Harold, we will go and attend to the matter at once."

CHAPTER FIFTH

CAPTAIN RAYMOND'S very kind invitation proved scarcely less agreeable to Mr. and Mrs. Dinsmore than to their younger friends and relatives, and their acceptance was telephoned to Woodburn before the Sunnyside party had left for their homes. All heard it with satisfaction, for Grandpa and Grandma Dinsmore were pleasant traveling companions. Some lively chat followed in regard to needed preparations for the trip, and in the midst of it, a servant came in with the afternoon mail.

The captain distributed it, and among Max's portion was a document of official appearance. Evelyn noted it with a look of apprehension, and she drew nearer to her young husband's side.

"Orders, my son?" asked the captain when Max had opened it and glanced over the contents.

"Yes, sir. It says am to go immediately to Washington upon the expiration of my leave, which will be about the time the rest of you set sail in the *Dolphin*."

The announcement seemed to put quite a damper upon the previous high spirits of the little company, and there were many expressions of disappointment and regret.

"Well," said Chester, getting on his feet as he spoke, "I must go home now. There is a little matter in regard to one of my cases that must be attended to at once, since I am likely to leave the neighborhood so soon."

"And if my husband goes, I must go, too," said Lucilla in a lively tone, rising and taking up the wrap she had thrown off on coming into the warm room.

"It is near the dinner hour. Would it be better for you to stay, all of you, and dine with us?" asked the captain.

All thanked him, but, declined, each having some special reason for wishing to go home at that particular time.

"Well, come in and share a meal with us all whenever you will," said the captain. "I think you know, one and all, that you are very heartily welcome."

"Yes, father, we do," said Max. "We are always glad when you care to breakfast, dine, or sup with us."

"Any of us but papa?" asked Ned.

"Yes, indeed, all of you from Mamma Vi down," laughed Max, giving the little fellow an affectionate clap on the shoulder as he passed him on his way out to the hall.

"Yes, Ned, each one of you will always be a most welcome visitor," said Chester.

"Indeed you will. You may be very sure of that," added Lucilla and Eva.

"So sure are we of that, that you need not be surprised to see any of us at any time," laughed Violet. "Nor will we be surprised or grieved to see any or all of you at any time."

"No, indeed! I want my daughters—and sons also—all to feel entirely at home always in their father's house," the captain said with his very genial smile.

"Thank you, father dear, and don't forget that Sunnyside is one of your homes, and we are always ever so glad to open its doors to you," said Lucilla, going to him and holding up her face for a kiss, which he gave with his usual warmth of affection.

"And not Lu's side only, but ours as well," added Evelyn, holding out her hand and looking lovingly into his face.

He took the hand, drew her closer to him, and gave her a caress as affectionate as that he had just bestowed upon Lucilla.

The rest of the good-byes were quickly said, and both young couples were wending their homeward way. They were all in a thoughtful mood, and the short walk was taken in almost unbroken silence.

Eva's heart was truly full at the thought of the approaching separation from her young husband. How could she bear it? He seemed almost all the world to her, now that they had been for four weeks such close companions. Life without his presence would be lonely and desolate indeed. She passed up the stairway to their bedroom, while he paused in the hall below to remove his overcoat and hat. Her eyes were full of tears, as she disposed of her wraps. She then crossed the room to her mirror to see that her dress and hair were in perfect order.

"No improvement needed, my own love, my darling," Max said, coming up behind her and passing an arm about her waist.

At that, she turned and hid her face upon his broad chest.

"Oh, Max, my husband," she sobbed. "How can I live away from you? You are now more than all the world to me."

"As you are to me, dear love. It is hard to part, but we will hope to meet again soon. In the meantime, let us write to each other every day. And as there is no war now, you need not feel that your husband is in any special danger."

"Yes, thank God for that," she said, "and that we may know that we are both in His kind care and keeping wherever we are."

"Surely you will be less lonely than you were before our marriage. Father claims you as his daughter, and Chester and little Ned are your brothers—Lu and Gracie your sisters."

"Yes, oh, yes. I have a great deal to be thankful for, but you are to me a greater blessing than all the world."

"As you are to me, dearest," was his response, as he held her close to his heart, pressing warm kisses upon cheek and brow and lip.

Meanwhile, on the other side of the hall, Chester and Lucilla were chatting about the captain's plan for a winter trip.

"I think it will be just delightful, Chester," she said, "since I am to have you along. I am so glad you are going, sorry as I am that ill health makes it necessary."

"Yes, my dear," he returned with a smile. "I am fortunate, indeed, in having so loving a wife and so kind and able a father-in-law. I am truly sorry that I must leave some important business matters to which I should give attention promptly and in person, but I intend to put that care aside and enjoy our holiday as fully as possible. I heartily wish Max could go with us. I think it would almost double the pleasure of the trip."

"As I do," responded Lucilla with a sigh, "but it seems one can never have all one wants in this world. I doubt if it would be good for us if we could."

"No, it assuredly would not. Now, my dear, I am going down to the library to look at some papers connected with one of my cases and shall be busy over them until the call to dinner."

The next few days were busy ones with those who were to have a part in the southern trip of the *Dolphin*. Woodburn and Sunnyside were to be left in the care of Christine and Alma with a sufficient number of servants under them to keep everything in order.

Max went with the others in the yacht, spent a half-hour there, then bade a very sad good-bye. He went ashore and took a train for Washington. It was Eva's first parting from her husband, and she shut herself into her stateroom for a cry to relieve her pent up feelings of grief and loneliness. But presently there was a gentle tap at the door, and Elsie Raymond's sweet voice asked, "Sister Eva, dear, don't you want to come on deck with me and see them lift the anchor and start the *Dolphin* on her way?"

"Yes, dear little sister. Thank you for coming for me," replied Evelyn, opening the door.

"All the rest of us were there, and I thought you would like to be there, too," continued the little girl, as they passed through the salon and on up the stairway.

"Yes, little sister, it is very kind of you to think of me."

"But I wasn't the only one. Everybody seemed to be thinking of you and looking around for you. So I asked papa if I should come for you, and he said yes."

"It was very kind of both him and you, little sister Elsie," Eva said with a smile. "Our dear father is always kind, and I am very glad to be his daughter."

"So am I," returned Elsie with a happy little laugh. "I think he's the dearest, kindest father that ever was made."

They had just reached the deck at that moment, and as they stepped upon it they caught sight of Harold and Gracie standing near, looking smilingly at them. They were pleased with Elsie's tribute to her father, which they had accidentally overheard.

"Oh, Uncle Harold, you'll take Sister Eva to a good place to see everything from. Won't you?" exclaimed Elsie.

"Yes, little niece, the everything you mean," he returned laughingly. "There is room for us all. Come this way," he added and led them to that part of the deck where the other passengers were grouped together.

There they were greeted with kindness and given a good place for seeing all the preparations for starting the vessel on her way to the Bermudas. She was soon moving swiftly in that direction, and, a cool breeze having sprung up, her passengers left the deck for the warmer and more comfortable salon.

"Elsie and Ned, wouldn't you two like your grandma to tell you something about the islands we are going to?" asked Mrs. Travilla, the two little ones being, as usual, quite near her.

"Yes, indeed, grandma!" both answered in eager tones, seating themselves one on each side of her. "I heard papa say it wouldn't be a very long voyage we would take at the start, because the Bermudas were only about six hundred miles away from our coast," said Elsie. "They belong to England. Don't they, grandma?"

"Yes, but they were named for a Spaniard, Bermudez, who first sighted them in 1527. They are also called Somers' Isles after Sir George Somers, an Englishman, who was shipwrecked there in 1609. That was what led to their colonization from Virginia—two years later, when the colony was itself only four years old."

"Are they big islands, grandma? And are there very many of them?" asked Ned.

"No, there are perhaps five hundred of them, but the whole group measures only about twelve thousand acres in all. They occupy a space only about twenty miles long by six broad."

"Then the group can't be worth very much, then, I suppose."

"They are valuable because their situation makes then a natural fortress that can hardly be overrated. They form a bond of union between two great divisions of British America—on each side of them is a highway between the Gulf of Mexico and the North Atlantic. There are many picturesque creeks and bays, large and deep. The water is so clear it reveals, even to its lowest depths, the many varieties of fish sporting among the coral rocks and all of the beautifully variegated shells."

"It has a warm climate. Hasn't it, grandma?" asked little Elsie. "I think that is why we are going there."

"Yes, the climate is said to be like that of Persia with the addition of a constant sea breeze."

"I shall like that," responded the little girl with satisfaction. "But what kind of people live on the islands, grandma?"

"A good many whites live there and still more colored people."

"Slaves, grandma?" asked Ned.

"No. The islands belong to England. Years ago, thanks to Mr. Wilberforce and others, the British abolished slavery in all their dominions."

"What are the names of some of them, grandma? The islands, I mean."

"The largest, which is fifteen miles long, is called Bermuda. St. George is three and a half miles long and is the military station of the colony. It commands the entrance of the only passage for large vessels. Its landlocked haven and the narrow and intricate channel leading into it are defended by strong batteries."

"You have been there. Haven't you, grandma?"

"Yes, years ago," she said with a sigh, thinking of the beloved partner of her life who had been with her then and there.

"Your Grandpa Dinsmore and I were there at the same time," remarked Grandma Dinsmore, sitting near, and she went on to give a graphic account of scenes they had witnessed there. Mr. Dinsmore presently joined in a way to make it interesting to the children.

CHAPTER SIXTH

GRANDPA DINSMORE had hardly finished his reminiscences of his former visits to the Bermudas when a sailor lad came down the companionway with a message from the captain—an invitation to any and all of his passengers to come up on deck, as there was something he wished to show them. It was promptly and eagerly accepted by the young folks—somewhat more slowly and sedately by the older ones.

"What is it, papa? Have you something to show us?" queried Ned, as he quickly gained his father's side.

"Something lying yonder in the sea, my son, the likes of which you have never seen before," replied the captain, pointing to a large object in the water at some little distance.

"Ah, a whale!" exclaimed Dr. Travilla, who had come up on Ned's other side. "To what genus does he belong, captain?"

"He is a bottlenose, a migratory species confined to the North Atlantic. It ranges far northward in the summer, southward in the winter. In the early spring, they may be found around Iceland and Greenland, Western

Spitzbergen, in Davis Strait, and probably about Novaia Zemlia."

"Oh, do they like to live right in among the icebergs, papa?" asked Elsie.

"No, they do not venture in among the ice itself, but they frequent open bays along its margin, as in that way they are sheltered from the open sea."

The group gathered about the captain on the deck now comprised all his cabin passengers. Not one of them failed to be interested in the whales or to have some remark to make or some question to ask.

"This one seems to be alone," remarked Lucilla. "Do they usually go alone, papa?"

"No, they are generally found in herds of from four to ten. Many different herds may be found in sight at the same time. The old males, however are frequently solitary; though sometimes one of them may be seen leading a herd. These whales don't seem to be afraid of ships, swimming around and underneath them until their curiosity is satisfied."

"I suppose they take them—the ships—for a kind of big fish," laughed Ned.

"Why is this kind of whale called bottlenose, papa?" asked Elsie.

"That name is given because of the elevation of the upper surface of the head above the rather short beak and in front of the blow hole into a rounded abrupt prominence—like a bottle."

"Blow hole," repeated Ned, wonderingly. "What's that, papa?"

"The blow holes are their nostrils through which they blow out the water collected in them while they are down below the waves. They cannot breath under the water, but they must come up frequently to take in a fresh supply of air. But first they must expel the air remaining in their lungs before taking in a fresh supply. They send that air out with great force, so that it rises to a considerable height above the water, and as it is saturated with water vapor at a high temperature. The contact with the cold outside air condenses the vapor, and that forms a column of steam or spray. Often, however, a whale begins to blow before its nostrils are quite above the surface, and then some sea water is forced up with the column of air as well."

They were watching the whale while they talked. It followed the yacht with seeming curiosity. At this moment it rolled over nearly on its side, then threw its ponderous tail high into the air, so that for an instant it was perpendicular to the water. He then vanished from sight beneath the waves.

"Oh, dear," cried Ned, "he's gone! I wish he'd stayed longer."

"Perhaps he will come back and give us the pleasure of seeing him spout," said the captain.

"Do you mean throw the water up out of its nostrils, papa?" asked Ned. "Oh, I'd like that!"

"Ah, there's our call to supper," said his father, as the summons came at that moment. "You wouldn't like to miss that?"

"No, sir," returned Ned in a dubious tone. "But couldn't we let supper wait till the whale comes up and gets done spouting?"

"Perhaps some of the older people may be too hungry to wait comfortably," returned his father, "and the supper might be spoiled by waiting. But cheer up, my son. The whale is not likely to come up to the surface again before we can finish our meal and come back to witness his performance."

That assurance was quite a relief to Ned's mind. So, he went cheerfully to the table with the others and there did full justice to the viands.

No one hurried with the meal, but when they left the table it was to go upon deck again and watch for the reappearance of the whale. They had been there for but a moment when, to the delight of all, it came up, not too far away to be distinctly seen. At once, he began spouting—or blowing—discharging the air from its lungs in preparation for taking in a fresh supply. The air was sent out with great force, making a sound that could be heard at quite a distance, while the water vapor accompanying the air was so condensed as to form a column of spray. He made five or six respirations and then swam away and was soon lost to sight.

Then the company returned to the cabin as the more comfortable place, the evening air being decidedly cool. Ned seated himself close to his father, and, in coaxing tones, he asked for some more information about the whales.

"Are there many kinds, papa?" he queried.

"Yes, my son, a good many—more than you could remember. Would you like me to tell you about some of the more interesting ones?"

"Oh, yes, indeed, papa!" was the emphatic and pleased response, and the captain began at once.

"There are the whalebone or true whales, which constitute a single family. They have no teeth, but instead, horny plates of baleen or whalebone, which strain from the water the small animals upon which the whale feeds."

"Oh, yes, I know about whalebones," said Ned. "Mamma and sisters have that in their dresses. It comes out of the whale's mouth. Does it, papa?"

"Yes. It is composed of many flattened, horny plates placed crosswise on either side of the palate and separated from one another by an open space in the middle line. They are smooth on the outer side, but the inner edge of each plate is frayed out into a kind of fringe, giving a hairy appearance to the whole of the inside of the mouth when viewed from below."

"Whalebone or baleen is black. Isn't it, papa?" asked Ned.

"Not always. The color may vary from black to creamy white. Sometimes it is striped in both dark and light."

"Is there much of it in one whale, papa?"

"Yes, a great deal on each side of the jaw. There are more than three hundred of the plates, which, in a fine specimen, are about ten or twelve feet long and eleven inches wide at their base. As much as a ton's weight has been taken from a large whale."

"Is the baleen all they kill the whales for, papa?" asked Ned.

"Oh, no, my son! The oil is very valuable, and there is a great deal of it in a large whale. I've been told of one that yielded eighty-five barrels of oil."

"Oh, my! That's a great deal," cried Ned. "What a big fellow he must have been to hold so much as that."

"The whale is very valuable to the people of the polar regions," continued the captain. "They eat the flesh and drink the oil."

"Oh, papa. Drink oil!" cried Elsie with a great shudder of disgust.

"It seems very disgusting to us," he said with a smile, "but in that very cold climate it is an absolute necessity. It is needful in order to keep up the heat of the body by a bountiful supply of carbon."

"Whales are so big and strong, it must be very dangerous to go near them, I suppose," said Elsie with an inquiring look at her father.

"That is the case with some of the species," he said, "but not with all. The Greenland whale, for instance, is inoffensive and timorous, and it will always flee from the presence of man unless aroused by the pain of a wound or the sight of its offspring in danger. In that case, it will sometimes turn fiercely upon the boat in which the harpooners are who launched the weapon, and, with its enormous tail, strike it a blow that will shatter it and drive men, ropes, and oars high into the air. That Greenland whale shows great affection for both its mate and its young. When this whale is undisturbed, it usually remains at the surface of the water for ten minutes and spouts eight or nine times. Then it goes down for from five to twenty minutes and comes back to the surface to breath again. But when harpooned, it dives to a great depth and does not come up again for half an hour. By noticing the direction of the line attached to the harpoon, the whalers judge the spot in which it will rise and generally contrive to be so near it when it shows itself again, that they can insert another harpoon or strike it with a lance before it can go down again."

"Poor thing," sighed little Elsie. "I don't know how men can have the heart to be so cruel to animals that are not dangerous."

"It is because the oil, whalebone, and so forth, are so valuable," said her father. "It sometimes happens that a stray whale blunders into the shallow waters of the Bermudas, and not being able to find the passage through which it entered, it cannot get out again. So it is caught like a mouse in a trap. It is soon discovered by the people, and there is a great excitement. They are full of delight and quickly launch their boats filled with men armed with guns, lances, and other weapons that would be of little use in the open sea but answer their purpose in those shoal waters.

"As soon as the whale feels the sharp lance in its body, it dives as it would in the open sea, but the water is so shallow that it strikes its head against a rocky bed of the sea with such force that it rises to the surface again half stunned.

"The hunters take advantage of its bewildered condition to come close and use their deadly weapons until they have killed it. The fat and the ivory are divided among the hunters who took part in the killing, but the flesh is given to any one who asks for it."

"Is it really good to eat, papa?" asked Ned.

"Those who are judges of whale flesh say there are three qualities of meat in every whale — the best resembling mutton, the second similar to pork, and the third resembling beef."

"The whales are so big and strong. Don't they ever fight back when men try to kill them, papa?" asked Elsie.

"Yes," he replied, "sometimes a large whale will become belligerent and is then a fearful antagonist, using its enormous tail and huge jaws with fearful effect. I have heard of one driving its lower jaw entirely through the plankings of a stout whaling boat and of another that destroyed nine boats in succession. Not only boats but even ships have been sunk by the attack of an infuriated old bull cachalot. An American ship, the *Essex*, was destroyed by the vengeful fury of a cachalot, which accidentally struck itself against the keel. Probably it thought the ship was a rival whale. It retired to a short distance then charged full at the vessel, striking it one side of the bows and crushing beams and planks like straws. There were only a few men on board at the time, most of the crew being in the boats engaged in chasing whales. When they returned to their ship, they found her fast sinking, so that they had barely time to secure a scanty stock of provisions and water. Using these provisions as economically as they could, they made for the coast of Peru, but only three lived to reach there, and they were found lying senseless in their boat, which was drifting at large in the ocean."

"It is a wonder to me that any one is willing to go whaling when they may meet with such dreadful accidents," said Evelyn.

"I suppose it must be very profitable to tempt them to take such risks," remarked Chester.

"It is quite profitable," said the captain. "A single whale often yields whalebone and blubber to the value of thirty-five hundred or four thousand dollars."

"I should think that might pay very well, particularly if they took a number."

"Our whale fishing is done mostly by the New Englanders. Isn't it, papa?" asked Gracie.

"Yes," he said, "they went into it largely at a very early date—at first on their own coasts. But they were deserted by the whales before the middle of the eighteenth century. Then ships were fitted out for the northern seas, but for a number of years, the American whale-fishery has been declining because of the scarcity of whales and the substitutes for whale oil and whalebone that have been found. However, New Bedford, Massachusetts, is the greatest whaling port in the whole world.

"Now it is nearing your bedtime, my boy, and I think you have had enough about the whale and his habits for one lesson."

"Yes, papa, and I thank you very much for telling it all to me," replied Ned with a loving, grateful look up into his father's face.

CHAPTER SEVENTH

SOME TWO HOURS later, the captain was taking his usual evening walk upon the deck when Lucilla and Evelyn joined him.

"We feel like taking a stroll, father, and we hope you will not object to our company," remarked Evelyn, as they reached his side.

"I could not with truth say it was unpleasant to me, daughter," he returned with a smile, passing a hand caressingly over her hair, as she stood close at his side. "The fact is, I am very glad of the companionship of you both."

"And we are both thankful to hear you say it, I am sure," returned Lucilla in a sprightly tone and with a bright, loving look up into his eyes. "I'd be heartbroken if I thought my father didn't love me enough to care to have me near him."

"And I should be much distressed if I had any reason to believe my daughter didn't care to be near me. If Gracie were as strong and healthy as you are, it would double the pleasure to have her here with us. She has gone to her stateroom, I suppose, for the night."

"Yes, papa, and most of the others have retired to their rooms, too. Dr. Harold and Chester are playing a game of chess, and so they will hardly miss Eva and me."

"Perhaps not. So we will take our promenade undisturbed by anxiety about them," laughed the captain, offering an arm to each. It was a beautiful evening. The moon was shining in a clear sky and making a silvery pathway upon the waters.

"Where do you suppose Max is now, father?" asked Evelyn with a slight sigh.

"Probably in Washington. Though it is quite possible he may received his orders and gone aboard his vessel."

"And doubtless he is thinking of you, Eva, as you are of him," said Lucilla, speaking in low, tender tones.

"No doubt of it," said their father, "for he is very fond of his sweet, young wife—as we all are, daughter dear," he added, softly patting the small, white hand resting upon his arm.

"Dear father," she said with emotion, "it is so kind of you to give me the fatherly affection I have so missed and longed for in years past."

"And daughterly affection from you is an adequate return," he said pleasantly. "I expect to enjoy that in all this winter's wanderings by sea and land."

"Wanderings I am very glad to be allowed to share," she said, and they talked of the various places they expected to visit on this winter trip.

At length Evelyn, saying it was high time for her to join Gracie in the stateroom they shared together, said goodnight and returned to her cabin, but Lucilla delayed her departure a little longer. It was so pleasant to have her father all to herself for a bit of private chat before retiring for the night.

They paced the deck silently for a few moments. Then she said, "Father, I have thought a good deal of the talk we had in our Bible lesson some time ago about the second coming of Christ. Do you think it—His coming—is very near, papa?"

"It may be, daughter. The signs of the times seem to indicate its approach. Jesus said, 'Of that day and hour knoweth no man, no, not the angels of heaven, but My Father only.' He has given us signs, however, by which we may know that it is near. Judging by them we may, I think, know that it is not very far off now."

"Then, papa, doesn't it seem as if we ought to be busied with religious duties all the time?"

"I think whatever duties the Lord gives us in His Providence may, in some sense, be called religious duties—for me, for instance, the care of wife, children, and dependents. We are to go on with household and family duties and those to the poor and needy in our neighborhood. We are also to take such part as we can in the work of the church at home and for foreign missions and so forth. We are to do all of this, remembering His command, 'Occupy till I come,' and endeavoring to be fully ready to meet Him with joy when He does come."

"And isn't a very important part of that trying to win souls to Christ?"

"It is, indeed, and 'he that winneth souls is wise.' Leading a truly Christlike life may often win them to join us in being His disciples, even though we refrain from any word of exhortation. Though there are also times when we should not refrain from giving them also."

"As you did to me, father," she said with a loving look up into his face. "Oh, I shall try to be a winner of souls. The Bible makes the way clear, again and again, in a very few words. You know it tells us Jesus said to Nicodemus, 'God so loved the world, that He gave His only begotten Son, that whosoever believeth in Him should not perish, but have everlasting life.'"

"Yes, and Peter said to Cornelius and his kinsmen and friends after telling them of Jesus, 'To Him giveth all the prophets witness, that through His name whosoever believeth in Him shall receive remission of sins.' And Paul and Silas, when asked by the jailer, 'Sirs, what must I do to be saved?' replied, 'Believe on the Lord Jesus Christ, and thou shalt be saved.' Salvation is God's free gift without money and without price. One must believe in His divinity, His ability and willingness to save, taking salvation at His hands as a free, unmerited gift. But now, dear child," he added, taking her in his arms, "it is time for you and that not very strong husband of yours to be seeking your nest for the night. 'The Lord bless thee, and keep thee; the Lord make

His face shine upon thee, and be gracious unto thee, and give thee peace,'" he added in solemn tones, laying a hand tenderly upon her head as he spoke.

"Thank you, dear father," she said in tones half-tremulous with emotion, "I do so love that blessing from your lips. And Chester and I both think I have the best father in the world."

"It is pleasant to have you think that," he returned with a smile and another caress. "But no doubt there are many fathers in the world quite as good, kind, and affectionate as yours. Perhaps if my daughters were less affectionate and obedient than they are, they might find their father more stern and severe. Now, goodnight, and may you have peaceful sleep undisturbed by troubled dreams."

Chapter Eighth

THE NEXT MORNING was bright and clear. They found the air so much warmer than that which had been left behind on their own shores that one and all repaired to the deck after breakfast and preferred to remain there during the greater part of the day. Mr. Horace Dinsmore, his wife, and daughter were sitting near together, and the ladies were occupied with some crocheting. Mr. Dinsmore held a book in hand, which he did not seem to be reading, when Elsie and Ned Raymond, who had been gamboling about the deck, came dancing up to them with a request for "more about Bermuda."

"You don't want to be surprised at all by the pretty things you will see there, eh?" queried their grandpa.

"No, sir. We want to hear about them first and see them afterward, if it isn't troubling you too much," said Elsie with a coaxing look up into his face.

"Well, considering that you two are my very own great-grandchildren, I think I must search my memory for something interesting on the subject. There are many picturesque creeks and bays. There are four pretty large islands—Bermuda being fifteen miles long. The strange shapes of the islands and the number of spacious lagoons make it necessary to travel about them almost entirely in boats, which is very pleasant, as you glide along under a beautiful blue sky and through waters so clear that you can see all the way to the bottom and all fish besides."

"Oh, I shall like that!" exclaimed Elsie. "Are the fish handsome, too, grandpa?"

"Some of them are strikingly so," he replied. "One called the parrot fish is of a green color as brilliant as that of his bird namesake. His scales are as green as the fresh grass of springtime, and each one is bordered by a pale brown line. His tail is banded with nearly every color of the rainbow, and his fins are pink."

"Is he good to eat, grandpa?" asked Ned.

"No, his flesh is bitter and poisonous to man and probably to other fishes. So they let him well alone, but he is nice to look at."

"Well, I suppose he's glad of that," laughed Ned. "The more I hear about Bermuda, grandpa, the more glad I am that we are going there."

"Yes, and you may well be thankful that you have so good and kind a father and that he owns this fine yacht."

"Yes, sir, I am that. But I'd rather be his son than anybody else's even if he didn't own a thing but me."

"And I'm just as pleased to be his daughter," said Elsie.

"And certainly I to be his grandfather-in-law," added Mr. Dinsmore with a comically grave look and tone.

"Yes, sir. Grandpa Travilla would have been his—papa's, I mean—father-in-law if he had lived. Wouldn't he?"

"Yes, and he would be almost as old as I am. He was my dear, good friend, and I gave him my daughter to be his wife."

"That was you, grandma. Wasn't it?" asked Ned, turning to Mrs. Travilla.

"Yes, dear," she said with a smile and a sigh. "If he had stayed with us until now, you would have loved him as you do Grandpa Dinsmore."

"Yes, indeed, grandma," came softly and sweetly from the lips of both children.

There was a moment of subdued silence, then Grandpa Dinsmore went on.

"There are many pretty creatures to be seen in the waters about Bermuda. There is a kind of fish called angels, which look very bright and pretty. They have a beautiful blue stripe along the back and long streamers of golden yellow, and they swim very gracefully about. But they are not so good as they are pretty. They pester the other fishes by nibbling at them, and so, often, they get into a quarrel, fighting with a long, sharp spine that they have on each gill cover. It makes ugly wounds with this spine on those they are fighting.

"Among the outer reefs we will, perhaps, see a speckled moray. He looks like a common eel, except that his body is dark green flecked with bright yellow spots, which makes him quite a handsome fellow. There is a fish the Bermuda fishermen call the Spanish hogfish, and when asked why they give it that name, they say, 'Why, sir, you see, it lazes around just like a hog and carries the Spanish colors.'"

"Spanish colors? What are they, grandpa?" queried Ned.

"The fish," said Mr. Dinsmore, "is brownish red from his head to the middle of his body, and from there to the end of his tail is a bright yellow. Those are the colors of the Spanish flag."

"I'm glad we are going to Bermuda," remarked Elsie with a happy little sigh. "I'm sure there must be a great deal there worth seeing."

"And your father is just the kind of man to help you to see all such things," responded Mr. Dinsmore.

"Yes, sir," said Elsie, "papa never seems to think it too much trouble to do anything to give us pleasure."

"Ah, what father would, if he had such a dear little girl and boy as mine?" queried a manly voice just behind them, while a gentle hand was laid caressingly on Elsie's head.

"Oh, papa, I didn't know you were so near," she exclaimed with a laugh and a blush. "Won't you sit down with us? Grandpa Dinsmore has been telling us some very interesting things about Bermuda."

"And papa can probably tell some that will be more interesting," remarked Mr. Dinsmore, as the captain took possession of Elsie's seat and drew her to one upon his knee.

That suited the little maid exactly. In her own opinion, no seat was more desirable than her papa's knee.

"Now, papa, we're ready to hear all you know about Bermuda," said Ned with a look of eager interest in what his father had to share.

"Perhaps you are more ready to hear than I am to tell," the captain answered with an amused smile. "At any rate, I want, first, to hear what you have been told, lest I should waste my time and strength repeating it."

The children eagerly repeated what had been told them. The captain added a few more facts about the beautiful things to be seen in the clear Bermuda waters—the coral reefs and the plants and animals that cover them. Then the call to dinner came, and all left the deck for the dining salon.

Almost the whole party were on deck again immediately upon leaving the table. The older ones were scattered here and there in couples or groups, but Elsie and Ned sauntered along together chatting in low tones, as if not wanting to be overheard by the older people.

"Yes, I am sorry," sighed Elsie in reply to something her brother had said. "Christmas is such a delightful time at home, and, of course, we can't expect to have one here on the yacht."

"No," said Ned, brightening, "but, of course, we can give Christmas gifts to each other, if—if we get to Bermuda in time to buy things. I s'pose there must be stores there."

"Surely, I should think. I'll ask Mamma or papa about it."

"Have you any money?"

"Yes. I have two dollars I've been saving up to buy Christmas gifts. How much do you have?"

"Fifty cents. It isn't much, but it will buy some little things, I guess."

"Yes, of course, it will. But, oh, Ned, Christmas comes Monday. Tomorrow is Sunday. So we couldn't do any shopping, even if we were on the land, and we may as well give it up."

"Yes, but we are having a very good time here on the *Dolphin*. Aren't we, Elsie?"

"Yes, indeed! And it would be really shameful for us to fret and worry over missing the usual Christmas gifts and pleasures."

The two had been so absorbed in the subject they were discussing that they had not noticed an approaching step. But now a hand was laid on a shoulder of each, and their father's loved voice asked, in tender tones, "What on earth is troubling my little son and daughter? Tell your papa your worries, and perhaps he may find a way out of the woods."

"Yes, papa. They are not very thick woods," laughed Elsie. "It is only that we are sorry we can't have any Christmas times this winter or remember anybody with gifts, because we can't go to any stores to buy anything."

"Are you quite sure of all that, daughter?" he asked with a smile, smoothing her shiny hair caressingly as he spoke.

"I thought I was, but perhaps my father knows better," she answered with a pleased little laugh.

"Well, I think a man of my age ought to know more than a little girl of yours. Don't you?"

"Oh, yes, indeed! And I know my father knows many, many times more about all kinds of things than I do. Is there any way for us to get gifts for all these dear folks on the yacht with us, or for any of them, papa?"

"Yes, I remembered Christmas when we were getting ready to leave home, and I provided such gifts as seemed desirable for each one of my family to give to others. I will give you each your share tonight before you go to your berths, and you can decide how you will distribute them — to whom you will give each one."

"But, papa, I — was —" Elsie paused, blushing and confused.

"Well, dear child, what is it?" asked her father in gentle, affectionate tones.

"I was thinking, papa, that they could hardly be our gifts when you bought them and with your own money, not ours."

"But I give them to you, daughter, and you may keep or give them away, just as you like. That makes them your gifts quite as truly as if they had been bought with your own pocket money. Does it not?"

"Oh, yes, papa, so it seems to me, and I know it does since you say so," exclaimed Elsie joyously.

Ned joined in with, "Oh, that's just splendid, papa! You are the best father in the world! Elsie and I both think so."

"Well, it is very pleasant to have my children think so, however mistaken they may be," his father said with a smile and an affectionate pat upon the little boy's shoulder. "Well, my dears, suppose we go down at once and attend to these matters. It will be better now than later, I think, and not so likely to keep you from getting to sleep in good season tonight."

The children gave an eager, joyful assent, and their father led them down to the stateroom occupied by Violet and himself. Opening a trunk there, he brought to light a quantity of pretty things—ribbons, laces, jewelry, books, and pictures along with cards with the names of the intended recipients to be attached to the gifts, as the young givers might see fit.

That work was undertaken at once, their father helping them in their selection and attaching the cards to them. It did not take very long, and they returned to the deck in merry spirits.

"For what purpose did you two children take papa down below? Or was it he who took you?" asked Lucilla, laughingly.

"I think it was papa who took us," said Elsie, smiling up into his face as she spoke. "Wasn't it, my dear papa?"

"Yes," he said, "and whoever asks about it may be told it was father's secret conference."

"Oh," cried Lucilla, "it is a secret then, is it? I don't want to pry into other people's affairs. So I withdraw my question."

"Perhaps papa intends to take his other children—you and me, Lu—down in their turn," remarked Gracie laughingly, for she was sitting near her father and had overheard the bit of chat.

"I really had not thought to do so," said the captain, "but it is a good idea. Come, now, both of you," he added, leading the way. "I suppose you two have not forgotten that tomorrow will be Sunday and the next day Christmas?" he said, inquiringly, as they reached the salon.

"Oh, no, papa. You know you helped us, before we left home, in selecting gifts for Mamma Vi and the children and others," said Gracie. "But how are we going to keep Christmas here on the yacht?"

"Pretty much as if we were at home on the land," he answered, smiling. "There is a Christmas tree lying down in the hold. I intend to have it set up here early Monday morning, and some of the early risers can trim it before the late ones are out of bed. Then it can be viewed, and the gifts distributed when all are ready to take part in the work and fun. If you wish I will show you the gifts I have prepared for my family—not including yourselves," he interpolated with a smile, "and our guests, servants, and crew here."

The offer was gladly accepted, and the gifts viewed with great interest and pleasure, the girls chatting meanwhile with affectionate and respectful familiarity with their beloved father.

"I like your plan, father, very much indeed," said Lucilla. "And as it is easy and natural for me to wake and rise early, I should like to help with the trimming of the tree, if you are willing."

"Certainly, daughter, I shall be glad to have you help and to put the gifts intended for you on afterward," he added with a smile.

"Yes, sir. Perhaps your daughters may treat you in the same way," she returned demurely. "I suppose you would hardly blame them for following your example?"

"I ought not to, since example is said to be better than precept. We will put these things away now, go back to our friends on deck, and try to forget gifts until Christmas morning."

CHAPTER NINTH

As on former voyages of the *Dolphin*, Sabbath day was kept religiously by all on board the vessel. Religious services—prayer, praise, and the reading of a sermon—were held on deck for the benefit of all, after which there was a Bible lesson led by Mr. Lilburn. The subject this day being Christmas Eve was the birth of Jesus and the visits of the wise men from the east and also the story of Bethlehem's shepherds and their angel visitors followed by their visit to the infant Savior.

The children went to bed early that night that—as they said—Christmas might come sooner. Then the captain, his older daughters, Chester, and Harold had a little chat about what should be done in the morning. The young men were urgent that their assistance should be accepted in the matter of setting up and trimming the tree. The girls also put in a petition for the privilege of helping with the work. To Lucilla their father answered, "You may, as I have said, for you are naturally an early bird, so that I think it cannot hurt you." Then turning to Gracie, "I hardly think it would do for you, daughter dear.

But we will let your doctor decide it," turning inquiringly to Harold.

"If her doctor is to decide it, he says quite emphatically, then, 'no,'" said Harold with a very lover-like look down into the sweet face of his betrothed. "She will enjoy the rest of the day much better for taking her usual morning nap."

"You and papa are very kind," returned Gracie between a smile and a sigh. "But I think you are a good doctor, so I will follow your advice and papa's wishes."

"That is right, my darling," responded her father, "and I hope you will have your reward in feeling well through the day."

"If she doesn't, she can discharge her doctor," said Lucilla in a mirthful tone.

"You seem inclined to be hard upon doctors, Lu," remarked Harold, gravely. "But one of these days you may be glad of the services of even such a one as I."

"Yes, that is quite possible. Even now I am right glad to have my husband under your care, and I'm free to say that if your patients don't improve, I don't think it will be fair to blame it — their failure — on the doctor."

"Thank you," he said. "Should you need any doctoring on this trip of ours, just call upon me, and I'll do the best for you that I can."

"I have no doubt you would," laughed Lucilla, "but I'll do my best to keep out of your hands."

"That being your intention, let me advise you to go at once to your bed," returned Harold, glancing at his watch. Then all said goodnight and dispersed to their rooms.

At early dawn, the three gentlemen were again in the salon overseeing the setting up of the Christmas tree. Then they arranged upon it a multitude of gifts from one to another of the *Dolphin's* passengers and some token of remembrance for each one of the crew. It was not in the kind heart of the captain ever to forget or neglect anyone in his employ.

The other passengers, older and younger, except Lucilla, who was with them in time to help with the trimming of the tree, did not emerge from their staterooms until the sun was up, shining gloriously upon the sea. But this morning their first attention was given to the tree, which seemed to have grown up in a night in the salon where they were used to congregating on mornings, evenings, and stormy days. All gathered around it and viewed its treasures with appreciative remarks. Then the captain, with Chester's and Harold's assistance, set about to distribute the gifts.

Every one had several and seemed well pleased with them. The one that gave Eva the greatest pleasure had been left for her by her young husband. It was an excellent likeness of himself set in gold and diamonds. She appreciated the beautiful setting, but the correct and speaking likeness was far more to her.

Near the tree stood a table loaded with fruits and confections of various kinds, very tempting in appearance. Ned hailed it with an expression of pleasure, but his father bade him let the sweets alone until after he had eaten his breakfast.

The words had scarcely left the captain's lips when a voice was heard, apparently coming from the skylight overhead, "Say, Pete, d'ye see them goodies piled up on that thar table down thar? My, but they looks temptin'."

"Yes," seemed to come from another voice, "wouldn't I like to git in thar and help myself? It's odd and real mean how some folks has all the good things and other folks have none."

"'Course it is. But, oh, I'll tell you. They'll be goin' out to breakfast presently. Then let's go down there where all the goodies is and help ourselves to 'em."

"Yes, let's."

Everybody in the salon had stopped talking and seemed to be listening in surprise to the colloquy of the two stowaways—for such they apparently were. But now Ned broke the silence, "Why, how did they get on board? Must be stowaways and have been in the hold all this time. Oh, I guess they are hungry enough by this time. So no wonder they want the candies and things."

"Perhaps Cousin Ronald can tell us something about them," laughed Lucilla.

"Acquaintances of mine, ye think, lassie?" sniffed the gentleman. "Truly, you are most complimentary. But I have no more fancy for such ones as they are than you have."

"Ah, well, now, cousin, I really don't imagine those remarks were made by any very bad or objectionable fellows," remarked Captain Raymond in a tone of amusement.

"No," said Mr. Dinsmore, "we certainly should not be hard on them if the sad fellows are poor and hungry."

"Which they must be if they have been living in the hold ever since we left our native shores," laughed Violet.

"Oh! Now I know! It was just Cousin Ronald and not any real person," cried Ned, dancing about in delight.

"And so I'm not a real person?" said Mr. Lilburn in a deeply hurt tone.

"Oh, Cousin Ronald, I didn't mean that," said Ned penitently, "only that you weren't two boys. You were just pretending to be."

At that everybody laughed, and Mr. Lilburn said, "Very true. I never was two boys and am no longer even one. Well, I think you and all of us may feel safe in leaving the good things on the table there when we are called to breakfast, for I am sure those fellows will not meddle with them."

The summons to the table had just sounded, and now it was obeyed by all with cheerful alacrity. Everybody was in fine spirits, the meal an excellent one, and all partook of it with appetite, while the flow of conversation was steady, bright, and mirthful.

They had their morning service directly after the meal and then went upon deck. To their surprise, they found they were in sight of Bermuda. They were glad to see it, though the voyage had been a pleasant one to all and really beneficial to the ailing ones, for whose benefit it was undertaken more particularly than for the enjoyment of the others. It was hoped and expected that their sojourn in and about the islands would be still more helpful and delightful than the journey there, and so indeed it proved.

They tarried in that neighborhood several weeks, spending most of their time on the vessel or in her small boats—many of the waterways being too narrow and shallow to be traversed by the yacht. And so they went from place to place on the land as well in a way to see all that was of any interest there.

CHAPTER TENTH

It was a lovely moonlight evening. The *Dolphin's* captain and all his family and passengers were gathered together upon the deck. It had been a day of sightseeing and wandering from place to place about the islands, and they were weary enough to fully enjoy the rest and quiet now vouchsafed them.

Captain Raymond broke a momentary silence by saying, "I hope, my friends, that you can all feel that you have had a pleasant sojourn in and about these islands?"

"Indeed, we have," replied several voices.

"I am glad to hear it," returned the captain, heartily. "Now the question is, 'Shall we tarry here longer or go on our southerly way to visit other places, where we will escape the rigors of winter in our more northern homes?'"

No one spoke for a moment. Then Mr. Dinsmore said, "Let the majority decide. I am perfectly satisfied to go on or to stay here, as you, captain, and they may wish."

"I echo my husband's sentiments and feelings," remarked Mrs. Rose Dinsmore pleasantly.

"And you, mother?" asked the captain, turning to Mrs. Travilla.

"I, too, am entirely willing to go or stay, as others of our party may wish," she replied in her own sweet voice.

"And you, Evelyn?" asked the captain, turning to her.

"I feel that it would be delightful either to go or to stay, father," she answered with a smile.

The others were quite as non-committal, but after some further chat on the subject it was decided that they would leave Bermuda the next morning, and, taking a southerly course, probably make Puerto Rico their next halting place.

As usual, Lucilla woke at an early hour. Evidently the vessel was still stationary, and anxious to see it start, she rose and dressed very quietly, lest she should disturb her still sleeping husband. She left the room and stole noiselessly through the salon up to the deck, where she found her father overseeing the lifting of the anchor.

"Ah, good morning, daughter," he said with a smile, as she reached his side. "You are an early bird, as usual," ending his sentence with a clasp of his arm about her waist and a kiss upon her upturned face.

"Yes, papa," she laughed. "Who wouldn't be an early bird to get such a token of love from such a father as mine?"

"And what father wouldn't be ready and glad to bestow it upon such a daughter as mine?" he responded, repeating his loving caress. "You have enjoyed your trip thus far, daughter. Have you not?"

"Yes, indeed, papa. We are bound for Puerto Rico now. Are we not?"

"Yes, I think that will be our first stopping place. Though perhaps we may not land at all, but merely sail around it and view it from the sea."

"Perhaps we may treat Cuba in the same way?"

"Very possibly. I shall act in regard to both as the majority of my passengers may wish."

The anchor was now up, and the vessel gliding through the water. The captain and Lucilla paced the deck to and fro, taking a farewell look at the receding islands and talking of the pleasure they had found in visiting them, particularly in exploring the many creeks and bays with their clear waters so full of beautiful shells and fish that were so different from those to be found in their land.

"I shall always look back with pleasure upon this visit to Bermuda, father," Lucilla said with a grateful smile up into his eyes.

"I am very glad you have enjoyed it, my daughter," he replied, "as I think every one of our party has. And I am hoping that our wanderings further to the south may prove not less interesting and enjoyable."

"Yes, sir, I hope so. I shall feel great interest in looking upon Cuba and Puerto Rico—particularly the first—because of what our men did and endured there in the late war with Spain. How pleasant it was that the Puerto Ricans were so ready and glad to be freed from the domination of Spain and taken into our Union."

Just then, Harold joined them, and with him came little Ned. Pleasant good mornings were exchanged. Then others of their party followed, two or three at a time, till all were on deck enjoying the sweet morning air and the view of the fast receding islands. Then came the call to breakfast followed by the morning service of prayer and praise. After that, they returned to the deck.

As usual, the children were soon beside their loved grandmother, Mrs. Elsie Travilla.

"Well, dears, we have had a very good time at Bermuda, haven't we?" she said, smiling lovingly upon them.

"Yes, ma'am," said Elsie. "Do you think we will have as good a time where we are going?"

"I hope so, my dear. I believe Puerto Rico is to be the first land we touch at. Would you like me to tell you something of its beauties and its history?"

"Yes, indeed, grandma," both children answered in a tone of eager assent, and she began at once.

"The name—Puerto Rico—was given it by the Spaniards and means, 'The Gateway of Wealth.' It was discovered by Columbus in 1493. It is about half as large as New Jersey. Through its center is a range of mountains called the Luquillo. The highest peak, Yunque, can be seen from a distance of sixty-eight miles. Puerto Rico is a beautiful island. The higher parts of the hills are covered by forests, and immense herds of cattle are pastured on the plains. The land is fertile, and they raise cotton, corn, rice, and almost every kind of tropical fruit."

"Are there any rivers, grandma?" asked Ned.

"Nine small ones," she answered.

"Are there any towns?"

"Oh, yes, quite a good many large ones. Ponce, the capital, has a good many thousands of inhabitants and some fine buildings. San Juan, too, is quite a large place. It stands on Morro Island, which forms the north side of the harbor and is separated from the mainland by a narrow creek called the Channel of San Antonio. At the entrance to San Juan's harbors is a lighthouse on Morro Point. It is 171 feet above the sea, and its fixed light is visible for eighteen miles over the water surrounding the islands."

"Oh," cried Ned, "let's watch out for it when we are coming near that."

"It will be very well for you to do so," his grandma said with a smile. Then she went on with her account of Puerto Rico.

"The island has much to recommend it. The climate is salubrious, and there are no snakes or reptiles. It has valuable minerals, too—gold, copper, lead, and coal. San Juan is lighted by both gas and electricity.

"The Spaniards were cruel to the Indians who inhabited Puerto Rico when Columbus discovered it. It is said that in a hundred years they had killed five-hundred thousand men, women, and children."

"Oh, how dreadful!" exclaimed Elsie. "And they also killed so many of the poor natives in Peru and in Mexico. I don't wonder that God has let their nation grow so poor and weak."

"The Puerto Ricans were growing tired of being governed by the Spaniards when we began our war with Spain to help the poor Cubans to gain their freedom," continued Grandma Elsie. "Our government and people did not know that, but they thought Puerto Rico should be taken from Spain along with Cuba. So, as soon as Santiago was taken, a strong force was sent against Ponce.

"The *Wasp* was the first vessel to arrive. It had been expected that they would have to shell the city, but as the *Wasp* steamed close to the shore, a great crowd of citizens could be seen gathered there. They were not behaving like enemies, and the troops on the *Wasp* were at a loss to understand what it meant. Therefore, the gunners stood ready to fire at an instant's warning, when Ensign Rowland Curtin was sent ashore bearing a flag of truce along with four other men.

"The citizens were cheering as if frantic with joy over their coming, and as soon as they landed, they overwhelmed them with gifts of tobacco, cigars, cigarettes, bananas, and other things."

"Oh, wasn't that very nice of them!" exclaimed Elsie. "I think they showed their good sense in preferring to be ruled by someone other than the Spaniards."

"As soon as the people could be calm enough to listen," continued Grandma Elsie, "Ensign Curtin announced that he had come to demand the surrender of the city and port and asked to see the civil or military authorities.

"Some of the civil authorities were there, but they could not surrender the city, as that must be the act of the military powers. There was a telephone at hand, and the ensign ordered a message sent to Colonel San Martin, the commandant, telling him that if he did not come forward and surrender the city in the course of half an hour, it would be bombarded.

"The garrison had been, and still even then were, debating what they should do, but as soon as they heard of this message, they began looting the stores and shops, cramming underwear and clothing upon their backs and in their trousers, to check and hold the bullets that they were certain the Americans would send after them, as they scampered off.

"Ensign Curtin went back to his vessel, and, soon after, Commander C. H. Davis of the *Dixie* was rowed ashore. There a note was handed him from Colonel San Martin, asking on what terms he demanded the surrender of the city. He answered that it must be unconditional. At the request of the commandant, however, he made the terms a little different. Then, the padded men of the garrison waddled out of town, leaving 150 rifles and more than fourteen thousand rounds of ammunition behind.

"Lieutenant Haines, commanding the marines of the *Dixie*, landed and hoisted the Stars and Stripes over the customs house at the port of Ponce, the onlookers cheering most heartily. After that, Lieutenant Murdoch and Surgeon Heiskell rode to the city, three miles distant, where the people fairly went wild with joy, dancing and shouting, 'Viva los Americanos. Viva Puerto Rico libre.'"

"Sensible folks I think they were to be so glad to get away from Spain and into the United States," remarked Ned with a pleased smile.

"Yes, I think they were," said Grandma Elsie. "For they were gaining liberty—freedom from a most oppressive tyranny."

She had begun her talk to the two children alone, but now quite a group had gathered about them—Dr. Harold Travilla and Gracie Raymond, Chester and Lucilla Dinsmore, and Mrs. Evelyn Raymond.

"I am very desirous to see Puerto Rico," said Harold. "It must be a garden spot—fertile and beautiful. As we draw near it, I mean to be on the lookout for El Yunque."

"What's that, uncle?" asked Ned.

"The highest point of land on the island. It is nearly four thousand feet high. The meaning of the name is 'the anvil'."

"Puerto Rico being in the Torrid Zone, it must have a very hot climate. The weather must have been oppressive for our troops, living in it in the very height of summer and the unbearable heat," remarked Gracie.

"Yes," said Grandma Elsie, "but the climate is more agreeable than that of Cuba or of many places farther north, because of the land breezes that prevail coming from both north and south."

"It is a beautiful and delightful island," remarked Harold. "I have often thought I should, some day, pay it a visit."

"Are we likely to land there?" asked his mother in her sweet-toned voice.

"I do not know, mother," he answered, "but I presume the captain will say that shall be just as his passengers wish."

"Yes, I am sure father will say we may all do exactly as we please," said Lucilla. "Go ashore, or stay quietly on the yacht while others go and return at will."

"It cannot now be the delightful place to visit that it was before the hurricane of last August," remarked Chester.

"No," said Grandma Elsie, "and I think I, for one, do not care to land on the island until they have had more time to recover from the fearful effects of that terrible storm."

"What mischief did it do, grandma?" asked Ned. "Were the people's houses destroyed, and people killed?"

"Yes, a great many," she answered with a sigh. "I have read that in one district it was estimated that the damage done to houses and crops would reach nine hundred thousand in gold. In the valley of the Rio Grande, over a thousand persons disappeared, and it is supposed that they were drowned by the sudden rise and overflow of the river."

"And you, mother, I know gave liberally to help repair the damages," said Harold.

"I was better able than many others who may have been quite as willing," she responded. "And I think I can do still more, if I find the need is still urgent."

"Yes, mother dear, you seem always ready and glad to help any one who needs it," said Harold, giving her a look full of proud, loving admiration.

Captain Raymond had drawn near the group just in time to hear Harold's last remark.

"Quite true, Harold," he said, "Who is to be the very happy recipient of mother's bounty this time?"

"We were talking of the unfortunate losses of the Puerto Ricans in last August's fearful storm," replied Harold. "Mother, as you know, has already given help and expresses herself as ready to do more if it is needed."

"And will do it, I know," said the captain.

"I hope, though, that my dear grandma won't give everything away and have nothing left for herself," said Elsie Raymond with a loving look up into her Grandma Elsie's face.

"I should not like to have her do that, either," said the captain with a smile. "But the Bible tells us, 'He that hath pity upon the poor, lendeth unto the Lord, and that which he hath given will He repay him again.'"

"A promise that none of us need be afraid to trust," said Grandma Elsie with a happy look and smile. "Do you think of visiting any part of the island, captain?"

"That shall be as my passengers wish," he replied. "We can consider the matter and talk it over while on our way there. My present plan is to go directly to San Juan. We may stay some hours or days there, those going ashore who wish and the others remaining on the vessel. We may make the circuit of the island, entirely or in part, keeping near enough to the land to gain a pretty good view of its beauties."

"Will this be your first visit to Puerto Rico, captain?" queried Chester.

"No, I paid it a flying visit some years ago, and then I went up the mountains to Caguas and visited the dark cave of Aguas Buenas."

"Did it pay?" asked Chester.

"Hardly. The outside journey, though difficult, did pay, but the darkness of the cave, the multitudes of bats flying in your face, and the danger of the guides' torches going out, leaving you unable to find your way out made the expedition anything but safe or pleasant. I shall never venture in there again, or advise a friend to do so."

"Are you going to take us to Cuba, too, papa?" asked Elsie.

"If my passengers wish to go there."

"Oh, I think they wil. This one does, anyhow," laughed the little girl.

"Don't you think it would be more pleasant to visit it after it has had time to recover from the war?" asked Lucilla.

"Perhaps papa will bring us a second time after that?" Elsie said with a smile up into his face.

"That is quite possible," he answered, returning the smile.

"Please, papa, tell us something about Cuba now, won't you?" pleaded Ned.

"Very willingly, if you all care to hear it," returned the captain. A general assent being given, he went on, "I think, much of it you will all understand better if told to you while you are looking upon the scenes where it occurred. However, since you wish it, I shall tell at least a part of the story now.

"Doubtless, you all know that Cuba was discovered by Columbus on October 28, 1492. He said of it at one time, 'It is the most beautiful land that eyes ever beheld,' and at another, 'Its waters are filled with excellent ports; its rivers are magnificent and profound,' and yet again, 'As far as the day surpasses night in brightness and splendor, it surpasses all other countries.'

"He found it beautiful not only along the shore where he first landed, but in the interior also — flowers, fruits, maize, and cotton in their vast abundance showed the fertility of the soil. And it was inhabited by a peaceful people who gave him and his men a glad welcome, imagining them to be superior beings and little dreaming how they were to later suffer at the hands of the Spaniards. Columbus describes them as tall and straight like the natives of North America of tawny complexion and gentle disposition, being easy to influence by their masters. They were a naturally indolent race, which was not strange, considering how easy it was for them to have a comfortable living with very little exertion. There was an abundance of wild fruits, and corn and cotton could be raised with little exertion. An abundance of fish could be easily obtained from the waters, and if they wanted meat, a little animal resembling a rat in appearance, but tasting like a rabbit, could be had for the hunting. So it would seem they lived easy, contented, and peaceful lives. Why the Spaniards should think they had a right to rob and enslave them, I will never know."

"Why, indeed!" exclaimed Lucilla. "The Indians—if able to do so—would have had just as good a right to go over to Spain and enslave them."

"But with the Spaniards, might made right," said Chester.

"But there were only a few Spaniards with Columbus and a great many natives on these islands," remarked little Elsie in a puzzled tone. "I wonder they didn't kill the Spaniards as soon as they began trying to make slaves out of them."

"At first," said her father, "they took the Spaniards to be a race of superior beings, and they gladly welcomed them to their shores. It would, doubtless, have been easy for them to crush that handful of worn-out men, and no doubt they would have if they could have foreseen what their conduct toward them would be. They mistook them for friends and treated them as such. One chief gave them a grand reception and feast amid songs and their simple music. Games, dancing, and singing followed, and then they were conducted to separate lodges and each provided with a cotton hammock. That proved a delightful couch to pass the night upon."

"The Spaniards took all that kindness at the hands of those poor things and repaid them with the basest robbery and cruelty," exclaimed Elsie.

"Yes," said her father, "they even repaid that most generous hospitality by seizing some of the youngest, strongest, and most beautiful of their entertainers and carrying them to Spain, where they were paraded before the vulgar gaze of the jeering crowd and then sold into slavery.

"One of their venerable chiefs gave to Columbus when he came the second time to the island a basket of luscious fruit, saying to him as he did so, 'Whether you are divinities or mortal men, we know not. You have come into these countries with a force, against which, were we inclined to resist, it would be folly. We are all, therefore, at your mercy. But if you are men, subject to morality, like ourselves, you cannot be unapprised that after this life there is another, wherein a very different portion is allotted to good and bad men. If, then, you expect to die, and believe, with us, that every one is to be rewarded in a future state according to his conduct in the present, you will do no hurt to those who have done none to you.'"

"That old chief was certainly a very wise man," remarked Chester.

"And how strange that the Spaniards could treat so shamefully such innocent and friendly people," said Evelyn.

"Papa, did that old king live long enough to see how cruel the Spaniards were to his people?" asked Elsie.

"That I cannot tell," replied the captain, "but by the time another ten years had passed by, the natives of Cuba had learned that the love of the Spaniards for gold was too great ever to be satisfied and that they themselves could not be safe with the Spaniards there. They were so alarmed that when Diego Columbus sent an armed force of three hundred men to begin to colonize Cuba, they resisted their landing. But they, the Indians, were only naked savages with frail spears and wooden swords, while the invading foes were old world warriors who had been trained on many a hard fought battlefield. They were armed with deadly weapons, protected by plate armor, and had bloodhounds to help in their cruel attempt to rob and subjugate the rightful owners of the soil. So they succeeded in their wicked designs. Hundreds of those poor Indians were killed in cold blood; others spared to a slavery worse than death. From being free men they became slaves to one of the most cruel and tyrannical races of the world. And they were not only abused there on their own island, but hundreds of them were taken to Europe and sold for slaves in the markets of Seville. That was done to raise money to pay the expenses of their captors."

"Why," exclaimed Ned, "the Spaniards treated them as if they were animals instead of people."

"Papa, were they — the Indians — heathen?" asked Elsie.

"They had no images or altars, no temples, but they believed in a future existence and in a god living above the blue-domed sky," replied the captain. "But they knew nothing of Jesus and the way of salvation, and it seems the Spaniards did not tell them of Him or give them the Bible."

"No," said Grandma Elsie, "Rome did not allow them the Bible for themselves."

"Are there a good many wild flowers in Cuba, papa?" asked Elsie.

"Yes, a great many of every color and tint imaginable. Flowers grow wild in the woods. The foliage of the trees is scarcely less beautiful, and their tops are alive with wild birds of brightly-colored plumage. I have been speaking of wild, uncultivated land. The scene is even more inviting where man has been at work transforming the wildwood into cultivated fields. He has fenced them off with stone walls, which have warm russet brown tints and are covered here and there with vines and creepers bearing bright flowers. The walks and avenues are bordered with orange trees in blossom and fruit at the same time, both looking lovely in their setting of deep green leaves. But you have all seen such tropical beauty in Louisiana."

"Yes, papa, and they are beautiful," said Elsie. "There must be a great deal worth seeing in Cuba, but I'll not care to land on it if you older people don't want to."

"Well, we will leave that question to be later decided," the captain said, smiling down into the bright, little face.

"I think I have read," said Evelyn, "that Columbus at first thought Cuba not an island but a part of the mainland?"

"Yes," replied the captain, "but the natives assured him that it was an island. On his second trip, however, in 1494, he reiterated his previous belief and called the land Juana, after Juan, the son of Ferdinand and Isabella. Afterward, he changed it to Fernandina in honor of Ferdinand; still later to Santiago, the name of the patron saint of Spain, after that to Ave Maria. But the name Cuba clung to the island and was never lost.

"The Indians there were a peaceful race. They called themselves Ciboneyes. They had nine independent caciques, or chiefs, and, as I believe I have already told you, they believed in a supreme being and the immortality of the soul in the life after death."

"Really, they seem to me to have been more Christian than the Spaniards who came and robbed them of their lands and their liberty," said Evelyn.

CHAPTER ELEVENTH

THE *DOLPHIN*, HER passengers, and crew reached Puerto Rico in safety, having made the voyage without any detention or mishap. The yacht lay in the harbor of San Juan for nearly a week, while its passengers made various little excursions here and there to points of interest upon the island. Then the yacht made its circuit, keeping near enough to the shore for a good view of the land, in which all were greatly interested — especially in those parts where there had been some fighting with the Spaniards in the late war.

"Now, father, you are going to take us to Santiago next, are you not?" asked Lucilla, as they steamed away from the Puerto Rican coast.

"Yes," he replied, "I am satisfied that you all take a particular interest in that place, feeling that you would like to see the scene of the naval battle and perhaps to look from a distance upon some of the places where there was fighting on land."

"It will be interesting," said little Elsie, "but, oh, how glad I am that the fighting is all over!"

"As I am," said her father. "But if it wasn't, I should not think of taking my family and friends to the scene."

"That was a big battle," said Ned. "I'm glad I'm going to see the place of the fight. Though I'd rather see Manila and its bay, because Brother Max had a share in that fight. Uncle Harold, you came pretty near having a share in the Santiago one, didn't you?"

"I was near enough to be in sight of some of it," said Harold, "though not so near as to some of the fighting on land."

"That must have been a very exciting time for you and your fellows," remarked Mr. Lilburn.

"It was, indeed. There was slaughter enough on land," said Harold. "Though we were pretty confident that victory would perch upon our banners in the sea fight, we could not hope it would prove so nearly bloodless for our side."

"The sea fight?"

"Yes, the fight on land was harder on our fellows, particularly because our unreasonable Congressmen failed to furnish for them the smokeless powder and Mauser bullets that gave so great an advantage to the Spaniards."

"Yes, indeed," said the captain, "That absolute freedom from smoke made it impossible to tell exactly from whence came those stinging darts that struck men down, and the great penetrating power of the Mauser bullet made them doubly deadly. They would cut through a palm tree without losing anything of their force, and, in several instances, two or more men were struck down by one and the same missile."

"It was very sad that that gallant young soldier, Captain Capron, was killed by that first volley," remarked Violet.

"Yes," said her mother, "I remember reading the account of his death and that he came of a family of soldiers. His father, engaged with his battery before the Spanish lines, left it for a brief time and came over to where the body of his son lay on the rank grass, looking for a moment on the still face. He said, 'Well done, boy, well done.' That was all, and he then went back to the battle."

"Yes, mother," said Harold in moved tones. "My heart aches all over again when I think of that poor, bereaved but brave father. Ah, war is a dreadful thing, even when undertaken from the good motive that influenced our people who felt so much sympathy for the poor, abused Cubans."

"The Americans are, as a rule, kind-hearted folk," remarked Mr. Lilburn, "and I doubt if there are any troops in the world superior to them in action—not even those of my own land."

"No," said the captain, "they were very brave fellows and good fighters, having seen service in our Northwest and Southwest, on the prairies, among the mountains, and on the Mexican frontier. So, war was no new thing to them, and they went about it calmly even in so unaccustomed a place as a tropical forest."

"Papa, Captain Capron wasn't instantly killed by that Mauser bullet. Was he?" asked Gracie.

"No, he was struck down early in the action and knew that his wound was mortal, but he called to a man near him to give him the rifle that lay by the side of a dead soldier. Then, propped up against a tree, he fired at the enemy with it until his strength failed, when he fell forward to die."

"What a brave fellow! It is dreadful to have such men killed," said Gracie, her voice trembling with emotion.

"Another man, Private Heffener, also fought leaning against a tree until he bled to death," said Harold. "Then there was Trooper Rowland, a cowboy from New Mexico, who was shot through the lungs early in that fight. He said nothing about it, but he kept his place on the firing-line until Roosevelt noticed the blood on his shirt and sent him to the hospital. He was soon back again. Seeing him, Colonel Roosevelt said, 'I thought I sent you to the hospital.' 'Yes, sir. You did,' replied Rowland, 'but I didn't see that they could do much for me there. So I came back.' He stayed there until the fight ended. Then he went again to the hospital. Upon examining him, the doctors decided that he must be sent back to the States, with which decision he was greatly disgusted. That night, he got possession of his rifle and pack, slipped out of the hospital, made his way back to his command, and stayed there."

"Perhaps," said Grandma Elsie, "you have not all read Marshall's experiences there. It happens that I have just been re-reading an extract that has interested me greatly. Let me read it aloud that you may all have the benefit of it. It is a description of the scene in the field hospital where badly wounded men lay crowded together awaiting their turns under the surgeon's knife. Shall I read it?"

There was a universal note of assent from her hearers, and she began: "'There is one incident of the day which shines out in my memory above all others now, as I lie in a New York hospital, writing. It occurred at the field hospital. About a dozen of us were lying there. A continual chorus of moans rose through the tree branches overhead. The surgeons, with hands and bared arms dripping, and clothes literally saturated with blood, were straining every nerve to prepare the wounded for the journey down to Siboney. Behind me lay Captain McClintock with his lower leg bones literally ground to powder. He bore his pain as gallantly as he had led his men, and that is saying much. I think Major Brodie was also there. It was a doleful group. Amputation and death stared its members in their gloomy faces.

"'Suddenly, a voice started softly:

My country, 'tis of thee,
Sweet land of liberty,
Of thee I sing.

"'Other voices took it up:

Land where my fathers died,
Land of the Pilgrims' pride—

"'The quivering, quavering chorus punctuated by groans and made spasmodic by pain trembled up from that little group of wounded Americans in the midst of the Cuban solitude. It was the pluckiest, most heartfelt song that human beings ever sang. There was one voice that did not quite keep up with the others. It was so weak that I did not hear it until all the rest had finished with the line, "Let Freedom ring."

"'Then, halting, struggling, faint, the voice repeated slowly, "Land—of—the—Pilgrims'—pride, Let Freedom—"

"'The last word was a woeful cry. One more son had died as died the fathers.'"

There was a moment's pause when Grandma Elsie had finished reading, and there were tears in the eyes of many of her listeners.

It was Harold who broke the silence.

"That battle of Guasimas was a total victory for our forces, but it was dearly paid for," he said. "Of the 964 men engaged, sixteen were killed and fifty-two wounded. Thirty-four of the wounded and eight of the killed were Rough Riders."

"And a scarcity of doctors seems to have caused great suffering to our wounded men," Grandma Elsie said with a sigh.

"Yes, there were too few of us," said Harold. "Through somebody's blundering, needed supplies were also scarce. I think our men were wonderfully patient, and it is hard to forgive those whose carelessness and inefficiency caused them so much unnecessary suffering."

"Yes, it is," said his mother. "War is a dreadful thing. How the people of beleaguered Santiago suffered during the siege and especially when they were sent out of it that they might escape the bombardment. Think of eighteen to twenty thousand having to take refuge in that little town, El Caney, which was foul with the effluvium from unburied mules and horses and even human victims of the battle. Houses were so crowded that they could not even lie down on the floors, but they had to pass their nights sitting on them. Food was so scarce that one small biscuit sold for two dollars, and seven dollars was refused for a chicken."

"It was dreadful, dreadful indeed!" commented Mrs. Lilburn.

"Yet not so bad as it would have been to let Spain continue her outrageous cruelty to the poor Cubans," said Evelyn.

"No," said Lucilla. "I should be sorry, indeed, to have to render up the account that Weyler and the rest of them will in the Judgment Day."

"I think he is worse than a savage," sighed Mrs. Lilburn. "I should think if he had any heart or conscience he would never be able to enjoy a morsel of food for thinking of the multitude of poor creatures—men, women, and children—he has starved to death."

⁂

CHAPTER TWELFTH

THE TRAVELERS WERE favored with pleasant weather on their voyage from Puerto Rico to Cuba. All were gathered upon deck when they came in sight of "The Pearl (or Queen) of the Antilles," or, "The Ever-Faithful Isle," as the Spaniards were wont to call it. They gazed upon it with keen interest—an interest that deepened as they drew near the scene of Schley's victory over the Spanish fleet.

Captain Raymond and Dr. Harold Travilla, being the only ones of their number who had visited the locality before, explained the whereabouts of each American vessel, when, on that Sunday morning of July third, that cloud of smoke told the watchers on the American ships that the enemy was coming out.

Every one in the little company had heard the battle described. Therefore, a very brief account, accompanying the pointing out of the progress of different vessels during the fight and where each of the Spanish ones came to her end, was all that was needed.

While they looked and talked, the *Dolphin* moved slowly along that they might get a view of every part of the scene of action on that day of naval victory in the cause of the down-trodden and oppressed Cubans.

That accomplished, they then returned to the neighborhood of Santiago, entering the narrow channel that gives entrance to its bay. They passed on into and around that, gazing on the steep hills that come down to the water's edge, on Morro, and the remains of all of the earthworks and batteries.

They did not care to go into the city, but they steamed out into the sea again and made the circuit of the island, keeping near enough to the shore to get a pretty good view of most of the places they cared to see. They traveled by day and anchored at night.

"Having completed the circuit of Cuba, where do we go next, captain?" asked Mr. Dinsmore, as the party sat on deck in the evening of the day on which they had completed their trip completely around the island.

"If it suits the wishes of all my passengers, we will go down to Jamaica, pay a little visit there, and pass on in a southeasterly direction to Trinidad. Then perhaps, we shall go on to Brazil," Captain Raymond said in reply and asked to hear what each one thought of the plan.

Every one seemed well pleased, and it was decided that they should start the next morning for Jamaica. The vessel was moving the next morning before many of her passengers were out of their berths. Elsie Raymond noticed it as soon as she woke, and she hastened with her dressing that she might join her father on deck. She was always glad to be with him, and she wanted to see whatever they might pass on their way across the sea to Jamaica. The sun was shining, but it was still early when she reached the deck, where she found both her father and eldest sister. Both greeted her with smiles and caresses.

"Almost as early a bird as your sister, Lu," the captain said, patting the rosy cheek and smiling down into the bright eyes looking up so lovingly into his.

"Yes, papa, I want to see all I can on the way to Jamaica. Will we get there today?"

"I think we will if the *Dolphin* does her work according to her usual fashion. But what do you know about Jamaica, the island we are bound for, little one?"

"Not so very much, papa—only—she belongs to England. Doesn't she, papa?"

"Yes. Her name means, 'land of wood and water,' and she lies about ninety miles to the south of Cuba."

"Is she a very big island, papa?"

"Nearly as large as our state of Tennessee. Crossing it from east to west is a heavily timbered ridge called the Blue Mountains, and there are many streams of water which flow from them down to the shores. None of them is navigable, however, except the Black River, which affords a passage for small craft for thirty miles into the interior."

"Shall we find a good harbor for our *Dolphin*, father?" asked Lucilla.

"Yes, indeed! Excellent harbors are everywhere to be found. The best is a deep, capacious basin in the southwest quarter of the island. It washes the most spacious and fertile of the plains between the hill country and the coast. Around this inlet and within a few miles of each other are all the towns of any considerable size—Spanish Town, Port Royal, and Kingston."

"Is it a hot place, papa?" asked the little girl.

"On the coast, but it is much cooler up on those mountains I spoke of. The climate is said to be very healthful, and many invalids go there from our United States."

"They have earthquakes there sometimes. Have they not, father?" asked Lucilla.

"They are not quite unheard of," he replied. "In 1692, there was one that almost overwhelmed Port Royal. But that being more than two hundred years ago, need not, I think, add much to our anxieties in visiting the island."

"That's a long, long time ago," said Elsie, thoughtfully. "So I hope they don't have one while we are there. Is it a fertile island, papa? I hope they have plenty of good fruits."

"They have fruits of both the tropical and the temperate climates. They have spices, vanilla, and many kinds of food plants. They have sugar and coffee. They export sugar, rum, pineapples, and other fruits as well as coca, ginger, pimento, logwood, and cochineal."

"It does seem to be very fruitful," said Elsie. "Have they railroads and telegraphs, papa?"

"Two hundred miles of railroad and seven hundred of telegraph. There are coast batteries, a volunteer force, and a British garrison. There are churches and schools."

"Oh, all that seems very nice! I hope we will have as good a time there on Jamaica as we had in Bermuda."

"I hope so, daughter," he said. "Ah, here come the rest of our own little family and also your Uncle Harold."

Affectionate good mornings were exchanged. Then talk ran on the subject uppermost in all their minds—Jamaica—and what its attractions were likely to be for them.

"I have been thinking," said Harold, "that some spot on the central heights may prove a pleasant and beneficial place for some weeks' sojourn for all of us, the ailing ones in particular."

At that moment, his mother joined them, and he broached the same idea to her.

"If we find a pleasant and comfortable lodging place, I am willing to try it," she replied in her usual cheery tones.

At that moment came the call to breakfast, speedily responded to by all the passengers. Appetites and viands were alike good, and the chat was cheerful and lively.

The weather was clear and warm enough to make the deck, where a gentle breeze could be felt, the most agreeable lounging place and the best place to enjoy the view of the sea and any passing vessels.

As usual, the children presently found their way to Grandma Elsie's side and asked for a story or some information concerning the island toward which they were journeying.

"You know something about it, I suppose?" she asked the two young ones.

"Yes, ma'am. Papa was telling us this morning about the mountains, towns, and harbors and about the fruits and other things they raise," said Elsie. "But there wasn't time for him to tell everything. So won't you please tell us something of its history?"

"Yes, dear. Grandma is always glad to give you both pleasure and information. Jamaica was discovered by Columbus during his second voyage in 1494. The Spaniards took possession of it in the year 1509."

"Had they any right to, grandma?" asked Ned.

"No, no more than the Indians would have had to cross the ocean to Europe and take possession of their country. And the Spanish not only robbed the Indians of their lands but abused them so cruelly that is said that in fifty years the native population had entirely disappeared. In 1655, the British took the island from Spain, and some years later it was ceded to England by the Treaty of Madrid in 1670."

"And does England own it yet, grandma?" asked Elsie.

"Yes. There has been some fighting on the island, but things are going smoothly now."

"So that we may hope to have a good time there, I suppose," said Ned.

"Yes, I think we may," replied his grandma. "But haven't we had a good time in all our journeying about old ocean and her islands?"

To that question both children answered with a hearty, "Yes indeed, grandma."

CHAPTER THIRTEENTH

THE NEXT MORNING found the *Dolphin* lying quietly at anchor in the harbor in the inlet around which are the principal towns of the island of Jamica—Spanish Town, Port Royal, and Kingston.

All were well enough to enjoy little excursions about the island in carriages or cars, and some weeks were spent by them in the mountains, all finding the air there very pleasant and the invalids evidently gaining in health and strength.

The change had been a rest for them all, but early in March they were glad to return to the yacht and set sail for Trinidad, which they had decided should be their next halting place. It was a pleasant morning, and, as usual, old and young were gathered upon the deck, the two children sitting near their grandmother.

"Grandma," said Elsie, "I suppose you know all about Trinidad, where papa is taking us now, and if it won't trouble you to do so, I'd like very much to have you tell Ned and me about it."

"I shall not feel it any trouble to do so, little granddaughter," was the smiling rejoinder, "and if you and Ned grow weary of the subject before

I am through telling you about it, you have only to say so, and I will stop.

"Trinidad is the most southerly of the West India Islands and belongs to Great Britain. It was first discovered by Columbus in 1498 and given the name of Trinidad by him, because three mountain summits were first seen from the mast-head. But it was not until 1532 that a permanent settlement was made there. In 1595, its chief town, San Josede Oruha, was burned by Sir Walter Raleigh, but the island continued in Spain's possession till 1797, when it fell into the hands of the British and it was made theirs by treaty in 1802."

"How large is it, grandma?" asked Ned.

"About fifty miles long and about thirty to thirty-five wide. It is very near Venezuela, only separated from it by the Gulf of Paria, and the extreme points on the west coast are only thirteen and nine miles from the points respectively. The channel to the north is called Dragon's Mouth; it is the deepest. The southern channel is shallow, owing to the deposits brought down by the Orinoco, and the gulf, too, is growing more and more shallow for the same cause."

"Are there mountains, grandma?" asked Ned.

"Yes, mountains not so high as those on some of the other Caribbean islands. They extend along the northern coast from east to west, and they have forests of stately trees and along their lower edges overhanging mangroves, dipping into the sea. There is a double-peaked mountain called Tamana, and from it one can look down upon the lovely and fertile valleys and plains of the other part of the island. There are some tolerably large rivers and several good harbors."

"Are there any large towns on it, grandma?" asked Ned.

"Yes. The chief one, called Port of Spain, is one of the finest towns in the West Indies. It was first built of wood and was burned down in 1808, but it has since been rebuilt of stone found in the neighborhood. The streets are long, wide, clean, well paved, and shaded with trees.

"San Fernando is the name of another town, and there are besides two or three pretty villages. Near one of them, called La Brea, is a pitch lake composed of bituminous matter floating on fresh water."

"I don't think I'd want to take a sail on it," said Elsie. "Trinidad is also a warm place. Isn't it, grandma?"

"Yes. The climate is hot and moist. It is said to be the hottest of the West India islands."

"Then I'm glad it is winter now when we are going there."

"Yes. I think winter is the best season for paying a visit there," said her grandma.

"I suppose we are going to one of the towns," said Ned. "Aren't we papa?" as his father drew near.

"Yes, to the capital, called Port of Spain. I was there some years ago. Shall I tell you about it?"

"Please do," answered both children, and a number of the grown people drew near to listen.

"It is a rather large place, having some thirty or forty thousand inhabitants. Outside the town is a large park, where there are villas belonging to people in good circumstances. They are pleasant, comfortable-looking dwellings with porches and porticoes and gardens in front or lawns with many varieties of trees—bread-fruit, oranges, mangoes, pawpaws—making a pleasant shade and bearing delightful fruits. There is also a great abundance of flowers."

"All that sounds very pleasant, captain," said Mr. Lilburn, "but I fear there must be some unpleasant things to encounter."

"Mosquitoes, for instance?" queried the captain. "Yes, I remember Froude's description of one that he says he killed and examined through a glass. Bewick, with the inspiration of a genius, had drawn his exact likeness as the devil—a long black stroke for a body, a nick for a neck, horns on the head, and a beak for a mouth, spindle arms, and longer spindle legs, two pointed wings, and a tail. He goes on to say that he had been warned to be on the lookout for scorpions, centipedes, jiggers, and land crabs, which would bite him if he walked slipperless over the floor in the dark. Of those he met none, but the mosquito of Trinidad was enough by himself, being, for malice, mockery, and venom of both tooth and trumpet without a match in this world."

"Dear me, papa, how can anybody live there?" exclaimed Gracie.

"Froude speaks of seeking safety in tobacco smoke," replied her father with a quizzical smile. "You might do that or try the only means of safety mentioned by him—hiding behind the lace curtains with which every bed is provided."

"But we can't stay in bed all the time, papa," exclaimed Elsie.

"No, but most of the time when you are out of bed you keep off the mosquitoes with a fan."

"And if we find them unendurable, we can sail away from Trinidad," said Violet.

"Perhaps we are coming to the island at a better time of year than Froude did with regard to the mosquito plague," remarked Grandma Elsie.

"Ah, mother, I am afraid they are bad and troublesome all the year round in these warm regions," said Harold.

"But we can take refuge behind nets a great deal of the time we are in the mosquito country and hurry to our floating home when we tire of that," remarked Violet.

"Ah, that is a comfortable thought," said Mr. Lilburn. "And we are fortunate people in having such a home as this to return to."

"Yes, we can all say amen to that," said Chester. Lucilla started the singing of *Home, Sweet Home,* and all the others joined in with obvious feeling.

The next morning found the *Dolphin* lying quietly in the harbor of the Port of Spain in the great shallow lake known as the Gulf of Paria, and soon after breakfast all went ashore to visit the city.

They enjoyed walking about the wide, shaded streets and park, gazing with great interest upon the strange and beautiful trees, shrubs, and flowers. There were bread-fruit trees, pawpaws, mangoes, and oranges in addition to large and beautiful flowers of many colors. Some of these friends had read Froude's account of the place and wanted to visit it.

From there they went to the Botanical Gardens and were delighted with the variety of trees and plants entirely new to them.

Before entering the place, the young people were warned not to taste any of the strange fruits, and Grandma Elsie and the captain kept watch over them lest the warning should be forgotten or unheeded — though Elsie was never known to disobey her father or mother, and it was a rare thing, indeed, for Ned to do so. They were very much interested in all they saw — the glen full of nutmeg trees among the rest. They were thirty to forty feet high with leaves like that of an orange folded one over the other, and their lowest branches swept the ground. There were so many strange and beautiful trees, plants, and flowers to be seen and admired that our friends spent several hours in those gardens.

Then they hired conveyances and drove about wherever they thought the most attractive scenes were to be found. They were interested in the cabins spread along the road on either side and overhung with trees—tamarinds, bread-fruit, orange, limes, citrons, plantains, and calabash trees. Out of the last named, the natives made their cups and water jugs.

There were cocoa bushes, too, loaded with purple or yellow pods. There were yams in the garden; cows in the paddocks also. It was evident that an abundance of good and nourishing food was provided to them with very little exertion on their part.

Captain Raymond and his party spent some weeks in Trinidad and its harbor—usually passing the night aboard the *Dolphin*—traveling about the island in cars or carriages, visiting all the interesting spots, going up into the mountains, and enjoying the view from thence of the lovely, fertile valleys and plains. Then they sailed around the island and anchored again in the harbor of Port of Spain for the night to consider and decide upon their next movement.

"Shall we go up the Orinoco?" asked the captain, addressing the company, as all sat together on the deck.

There was a moment of silence, each waiting for the others to speak. Then Mr. Dinsmore said, "Give us your views on the subject, captain. Is there much to attract us there or to interest and instruct? I am really afraid that it is a part of my geography in which I am rather rusty."

"It is one of the great rivers of South America," said the captain. "It rises in one of the chief mountain chains of Guiana. It is a crooked stream—flowing west, southwest, then southwest, then northwest, then north, north-east, and after that in an eastward direction to its mouth. The head of uninterrupted navigation is 777 miles from its mouth. Above that point there are cataracts.

"It has a great many branches, being joined, it is said, by 436 rivers and upward of two thousand streams. So, it drains an area of about 250,000 to 650,000 square miles, it is estimated. It begins to form its delta 130 miles from its mouth, by throwing off a branch that flows northward into the Atlantic. It has several navigable mouths, and the main stream is divided by a line of islands into two channels, each two miles wide. The river is four miles wide at Bolivar, a town which is more than 250 miles from the mouth of the river, and is 390 feet deep."

"Why, it's a grand, big river," said Chester. "We are much obliged for the information, captain. I had forgotten, if I ever knew, that it was so large and, with its many tributaries, drained so large a territory."

"Do you wish to visit it—or a part of it?" queried the captain. "How is it with you, Cousins Annis and Ronald?"

"I am willing—indeed, should prefer—to leave the decision to other members of our party," replied Mrs. Lilburn, and her husband expressed the same wish to let others decide the question.

"What do you say, Grandma?" asked Violet. "I think you look as if you would rather not go."

"And that is exactly how I feel—thinking of the mosquitoes," returned her Grandma Rose with a slight laugh.

"They certainly are very objectionable," said the captain. "I can't say that I am at all desirous to try them myself. And I doubt if they are more scarce on the Amazon than on the Orinoco. One traveler there tells us, 'At night it was quite impossible to sleep for the mosquitoes. They fell upon us by myriads and without much piping came straight to our faces as thick as raindrops in a shower. The men crowded into the cabins and tried to expel them by smoke from burnt rags, but it was of little avail, though we were half suffocated by the operation.'"

"That certainly does not sound encouraging, my dear," said Violet.

"The Amazon is a grand river, I know," said Harold, "but it would not pay to visit it under so great a drawback to one's comfort. I am very sure encountering such pests would be by no means beneficial to any one of my patients."

"And this one of your patients would not be willing to encounter them, even if such were the prescription of her physician," remarked Gracie in a lively tone.

"Nor would this older one," added Grandma Elsie in playful tones.

"Then we will consider the Orinoco as tabooed," said the captain. "I suppose we shall have to treat the Amazon in the same way, as it was at a place upon its banks that one of the writers I just quoted had his most unpleasant experience with mosquitoes."

"Well, my dear, if there is a difference of opinion and choice among us—some preferring scenery even with mosquitoes, others no scenery unless it could be had without mosquitoes—suppose we divide our forces. One set could go by land, and the other remain on board and journey on up the river."

"Ah! And what set will you join, little wife?" he asked with playful look and tone.

"Whichever one my husband belongs to," she answered. "Man and wife are not to be separated."

"Suppose we take a vote on the question and settle it at once," said Lucilla.

"A good plan, I think," said Harold.

"Yes," assented the captain. "Cousins Annis and Ronald, please give us your wishes in regard to the mosquitoes."

"I admire the rivers but not the mosquitoes, and I would rather do without both than have both," laughed Annis.

Her husband added, "My sentiments on the subject coincide exactly with those of my wife."

Then the question went round the circle, and it appeared that every one thought a sight of the great rivers and the scenery on their banks would be too dearly purchased by venturing in among clouds of blood-thirsty mosquitoes.

"I'm glad," exclaimed Ned. "I'm not a bit fond of mosquitoes—especially not of having them take their meals off me. But I'd like to see those big rivers. Papa, won't you tell us something about the Amazon?"

"Yes," said the captain. "It has two other names — Maranon and Orellana. It is a very large river and has a big mouth — 150 miles wide — and the tide enters there and goes up stream five hundred miles.

"From the wide mouth of the Amazon where it empties into the ocean, its water can be distinguished from the other — that of the ocean — for fifty leagues. The Amazon is so large and has so many tributaries that it drains 2,000,500 square miles of country. The Amazon is the king of rivers. It rises in the western range of the Andes and is little better than a mountain torrent till it has burst through the gorges of the eastern range of the chain. There it is overhung by peaks that tower thousands of feet above its bed. Within three hundred miles of the Pacific is a branch, Huallagais, large enough and deep enough for streamers, and a few miles farther down the Amazon is navigable for vessels drawing five feet. It grows deeper and deeper and more and more available for large vessels as it rolls on toward the ocean. The outlet of this mighty river is a feeder of the Gulf Stream. It is only since 1867 that the navigation of the Amazon has been open, but now regular lines of steamers ply between its mouth and Yurimaguas on the Huallaga."

"Are there not many important exports sent down the Amazon?" asked Mr. Dinsmore.

"There are, indeed," replied the captain, "and the fauna of the waters have proved wonderful. Agassiz found there, during five months, over thirteen hundred species of fish, nearly a thousand of them new, and about twenty genera. The Vacca marina, the largest inhabiting fresh waters, and the Acara, which carries its young in its mouth when there is danger, are the denizens of the Amazon."

"Oh," exclaimed Elsie, "I'd like to see that fish with its babies in its mouth."

"But I should be very sorry to have to carry my children in that way—even if the relative size of my mouth and my children made it possible," said her mother.

"Brazil's a big country. Isn't it, papa?" asked Ned of his father.

"Yes," said his father, "about as large as the United States would be without Alaska."

"Did Columbus discover it, and the Spaniards settle it, papa?" he asked.

"In the year 1500, a companion of Columbus landed at Cape Augustine, near Pernambuco. From there, he sailed along the coast as far as the Orinoco," replied the captain. "In the same year, another Portuguese commander driven to the Brazilian coast by adverse winds landed and, taking possession in the name of his monarch, named the country Terra da Vera Crux. The first permanent settlement was made by the Portuguese in 1531 on the island of St. Vincent. Many settlements were made and abandoned because of the hostility of the natives and the lack of means, and a Huguenot colony, established on the bay of Rio de Janeiro in 1555, was broken up by the Portuguese in 1567 when they founded the present capital, Rio de Janeiro.

"But it is hardly worthwhile to rehearse all the history of the various attempts to take possession of Brazil—attempts made by Dutch, Portuguese, and Spanish. The French invasion of Portugal in 1807 caused the royal family to flee to Brazil, and it became the royal seat of government until 1821, when Dom John VI went back to Portugal, leaving his eldest son Dom Pedro, as Prince Regent of Brazil.

"The independence of Brazil was proclaimed on September 7, 1822. On October twelfth, he was crowned emperor as Dom Pedro I. He was arbitrary, and that made him so unpopular that he found it best to abdicate, which he did in 1831 in favor of his son, then only a child. That boy was crowned in 1841 at the age of fifteen as Dom Pedro II."

"Gold is to be found in Brazil. Is it not, papa?" asked Gracie.

"Yes," he said. "That country is rich in minerals and precious stones. Gold, always accompanied with silver, is found in many of the provinces. In Minas-Geraes, it is especially abundant, and in that and two other of the provinces, diamonds are found. The opal, amethyst, emerald, ruby, sapphire, tourmaline, topaz, and other precious stones are more or less common."

"Petroleum also is obtained in one or two of the provinces, and there are valuable phosphate deposits on some of the islands," remarked Mr. Dinsmore, as the captain paused, as if he had finished what he had to say in reply to Gracie's question.

"Papa," asked Ned, "are there lions and tigers and monkeys in the woods?"

"There are dangerous wild beasts — the jaguar being the most common and formidable. There are other wild, some of them dangerous, beasts — the tiger cat, red wolf, tapir, wild hog, Brazilian dog or wild fox, capybara or water hog, paca, three species of deer, armadillos, sloths, ant-eaters, oppossums, coatis, water-rats, otters, and porcupines. Squirrels, hares, and rabbits are plentiful. There are many species of monkeys, too, and several kinds of bats — vampires among them. On the southern plains, large herds of wild horses are to be found. Indeed, Brazil can boast a long list of animals. One writer says that he found five hundred species of parrots and twenty varieties of hummingbirds. The largest birds are the ouira, a large eagle; the rhea, or American ostrich; and the cariama. Along the coasts or in the forest are to be found frigate birds, snowy herons, toucans, ducks, wild peacocks, turkey geese, and pigeons. Among the smaller birds are the oriole, whippoorwill, and the uraponga — or bell bird."

"Those would be pleasant enough to meet," said Violet, "but there are also plenty of most unpleasant creatures — snakes, for instance."

"Yes," assented the captain. "There are many serpents. The most venomous are the jararaca and the rattlesnake. The boa constrictor and the anaconda grow very large, and there are at least three species of cobra noted as dangerous. There are many alligators, turtles, and lizards. The rivers, lakes, and coast-waters literally swarm with fish. Agassiz found nearly two thousand species, many of them such as are highly esteemed for food."

"And they have big mosquitoes, too, you have told us, papa," said Elsie. "Many other bugs, too, I suppose?"

"Yes, big beetles, scorpions, spiders, many kinds of bees, sand-flies, musical crickets, destructive ants, the cochineal insect, and the pium, a tiny insect whose bite is poisonous and sometimes dangerous."

"Please tell us about the woods there, papa," said Ned.

"Yes. The forests of the Amazon valley are said to be the largest in the world, having fully four hundred species of trees. In marshy places and along streams, reeds, grasses, and water plants grow in tangled masses. In the forests, the trees crowd each other and are draped with parasitic vines. Along the coasts, mangroves, mangoes, cocoas, dwarf palms, and the brazil-wood are noticeable. In one of the southern provinces, more than forty kinds of trees are valuable for timber. On the Amazon and its branches, there are an almost innumerable variety of valuable trees—among them the itauba or stonewood, so named for its durability, the cassia, the cinnamon tree, the banana, the lime, the myrtle, the guava, the jacaranda, or rosewood, the Brazilian bread-fruit, whose large seeds are used for food, and many others too numerous to mention. Among others are the large and lofty cotton tree, the tall white-trunked seringa or rubber tree, which furnishes the gum of commerce, and three or four hundred species of palms. One of those is called the carnaubu palm. It is probably the most valuable, for every part of the plant is useful, from the wax of its leaves to its edible pith. Another is the piassaba palm, whose bark is clothed with a loose fiber used for coarse textile fabrics and also for brooms."

"Why, papa, that's a very useful tree," was little Elsie's comment upon receiving that bit of information. "Are there fruits and flowers in those forests, papa?" she asked.

"Yes, those I have already mentioned along with figs, custard apples, and oranges. Some of the European fruits—olives, grapes, and also fine watermelons are cultivated in Brazil."

"If it wasn't for the fierce wild animals and snakes, it would be a nice country to live in, I think," she said. "But, taking everything into consideration, I think I very much prefer our own country."

"Ah, is that so? Who shall say that you won't change your mind after a few weeks spent in Brazil?" returned her father with an amused look at his youngest daughter.

"You wouldn't want me to. I know, papa," she returned with a pleasant little laugh. "I am very sure you want your children to love their own country better than any other in the world."

"Yes, my child, I do," he said. Then turning to his older passengers and addressing them in general, "I think," he said, "if it is agreeable to you all, we will make a little stop at Pará, the maritime emporium of the Amazon. I presume you would all like to see that city?"

All seemed pleased with the idea, and it was presently settled that the city should be their next stopping place. They all enjoyed their life upon the yacht, but an occasional halt and visit to the shore made an agreeable variety.

CHAPTER
FOURTEENTH

THEIR SAIL ABOUT THE mouth of the Amazon was very interesting to them all and that up the Pará River to the city of the same name not less so. They found the city evidently a busy and thriving place. Its harbor, formed by a curve of the River Pará, there twenty miles wide, had at anchor in it a number of large vessels of various nationalities. The *Dolphin* anchored among them, and after a little while, her passengers went ashore for a drive about the city.

They found the streets paved and also macadamized. The houses had white walls and red-tiled roofs. There were some large and imposing buildings—a cathedral, churches, and the president's palace were the principal ones. They visited the public square and beautiful botanical gardens.

It was not very late in the day when they returned to the yacht, but they—especially Dr. Harold's patients—were weary enough to enjoy the quiet rest to be found in their ocean home.

"What a busy place it is," remarked Grandma Elsie, as they sat together upon the deck, gazing out upon the city and its harbor.

"Yes," said the captain, "Pará is the mart through which passes the whole commerce of the Amazon and its affluents."

"And that must, of course, make it a place of importance," said Violet.

"It was the seat of the revolution in 1833," remarked her grandfather. "Houses were destroyed, and lives lost—a great many of them—and grass grew in streets which before had been the center of business."

"Papa! Papa!" exclaimed Ned. "Look! There's a little boat coming and a man in it with some little animals."

"Ah, yes. Small monkeys, I think they are," Captain Raymond said, taking a view over the side of the vessel.

Then he called to a sailor that he wanted the man to be allowed to come aboard with whatever he had for sale. In a few moments, he was at hand carrying two little monkeys in his arms. He approached the captain and bowing low, hat in hand, addressed him in Portuguese. First, he said, "Good evening," then went on to tell that these were fine little monkeys—tee-tees, by name—which he had brought for sale. He went on to talk fluently in praise of the little creatures, which were about the size of a squirrel. The hair of their body and limbs was of a grayish olive with a rich golden hue on the latter. The under surface of the body was a whitish gray color, and the tip of the tail was black.

"Oh, how pretty. How very pretty!" exclaimed little Elsie. "Papa, won't you buy me one?"

"Yes, daughter, if you want it," returned the captain. "I know you will be kind to it, and that it will be a safe and pretty pet for you."

"Oh, papa, I'd like to have the other one, if I may!" cried Ned, fairly dancing with delight at the thought of owning the pretty little creature.

The captain smiled and said something to the man, speaking in Portuguese — a language spoken and understood by those two only of all on board the vessel.

The man answered, saying, as the captain afterward told the others, that he was very glad to sell both to one person, because the little fellows were brothers and would be company for each other.

Then a tee-tee was handed to each of the younger children. The captain gave the man some money, which seemed to please him, and he went away, while Elsie and Ned rejoiced over and exhibited their pets. They fed them and found a comfortable sleeping place for them for the night.

"What lovely, engaging little things they are!" said Grandma Elsie, as the children carried them away. "The prettiest monkeys I ever saw."

"Yes," said the captain, "they are of a very pretty and engaging genus of monkeys. We all noticed the beauty of their fur, from which they are called callithrix or 'beautiful hair.' Sometimes they are called squirrel monkeys, partly on account of their shape and size, and partly from their squirrel-like activity. They are light and graceful little creatures. I am hoping my children will have great pleasure in their company. They are said to attach themselves very strongly to their possessors and behave with a gentle intelligence that lifts them far above the greater part of the monkey race."

"I think I have read somewhere that they are good-tempered," said Grandma Elsie.

"Yes. They are said to be very amiable, anger seeming to be almost unknown to them. Did you not notice the almost infantile innocence in the expression of their countenances?"

"Yes, I did," she replied. "It was very touching and made me feel an affection for them at once."

"I have read," said Evelyn, "that that is a typical reaction when little creatures are alarmed. Sudden tears will come into their clear hazel eyes, and they will make a little imploring, shrinking gesture quite irresistible to any sort of kind-hearted, sympathetic people."

"I was reading about the tee-tees not long ago," said Mrs. Lilburn. "One thing I learned was that they had a curious habit of watching the lips of those who speak to them, just as if they could understand the words spoken, and when they become quite familiar, they are quite fond of sitting on their friend's shoulder and laying their tiny fingers on his lips, as if they thought in that way they might discover the grand mysteries of human speech."

"Poor little darlings! I wish they could talk," exclaimed Gracie. "I daresay they would make quite as good a use of the power of speech as parrots do."

"Possibly even better," said her father. "They seem to be more affectionate."

"Do they live in flocks in their own forests, papa?" Gracie asked.

"Yes," he replied, "so the traveler, Mr. Bates, tells us. When on the move, they take flying leaps from tree to tree."

"I am glad you bought those, papa," she said. "I think they will be a pleasure and amusement to us all."

"So do I," said Lucilla. "They are so pretty and graceful that I think we will all be inclined to pet them."

"So I think," said her father. "They seem to me decidedly the prettiest and most interesting species of monkey I have ever met."

"It really is very pleasant to see how delighted the children are with their new pets," said Grandma Elsie.

"Yes," the captain responded with a pleased smile. "I have no fear that either of them will ill-use them."

"I am sure they will be kind to them," said Violet. "They were much interested in the monkeys we saw as we went about the city. I saw quite a number of various species — some pretty large, but most of them small. There were some at the doors or windows of houses and some in canoes on the river."

"Yes, I think we all noticed them," commented her mother.

"Yes," said the captain. "I saw several of the midas ursulus, a small monkey which I have read is often to be found here in Pará. It is, when full grown, only about nine inches long, exclusive of tail, which is fifteen inches long. It has thick, black fur with a reddish brown streak down the middle of the back. It is said to be a timid little thing, but when treated kindly they become very tame and familiar."

"What do monkeys eat, papa?" asked Gracie.

"I have been told the cute little fellows are generally fed on sweet fruits, such as the banana, and that they are also fond of grasshoppers and soft-bodied spiders."

"They have some very large and busy ants in this country. Haven't they, father?" asked Evelyn.

"Yes," replied the captain. "Bates tells of some an inch long, stout in proportion, marching in single file through the thickets. They, however, have nothing peculiar or attractive in their habits, though they are giants among ants. But he speaks of another and far more interesting species. It is a great scourge to the Brazilians from its habit of despoiling the most valuable of the cultivated trees of their foliage. In some districts, it is such a pest that agriculture is almost impossible. He goes on to say that in their first walks, they were puzzled to account for mounds of earth of a different color from the surrounding soil. These mounds, some of them very extensive and some forty yards in circumference, were not more than two feet high. On making inquiries, they learned that those mounds were the work of the saubas — the outworks and domes which overlie and protect the entrances to their vast subterranean galleries. On close examination, Bates found the earth of which they were made to consist of very minute granules heaped together with cement so as to form many rows of little ridges and turrets. He learned that the difference in color from the earth around was due to the undersoil having been brought up from a considerable depth to form these mounds."

"I should like to see the ants at work upon them," said Gracie.

"It is very rare that one has the opportunity to do so," said her father. "Mr. Bates tells us that the entrances are generally closed galleries, opened only now and then when some particular work is going on. He says he succeeded in removing portions of the dome in smaller hillocks and found that minor entrances converged at the depth of about two feet to one broad, elaborately worked gallery, or mine, which was four or five inches in diameter."

"Isn't it the ant that clips and carries away leaves?" asked Evelyn.

"Yes, Bates speaks of that. He says it has long been recorded in books of natural history, and that when employed on that work their long procession looks like a multitude of animated leaves on the march. In some places, he found an accumulation of such leaves, all circular pieces about the size of a sixpence, lying on the pathway with no ants near it and at some distance from the colony. 'Such heaps,' he says, 'are always found to have been removed when the place is revisited the next day. The ants mount the trees in multitudes. Each one is a working miner, places itself on the surface of a leaf, and cuts with its sharp, scissor-like jaws. By a sharp jerk, it detaches the leaf piece. Sometimes they let the leaf drop to the ground, where a little heap accumulates until carried away by another relay of workers, but generally each marches off with the piece he has detached. All take the same road to their colony, and the path they follow becomes, in a short time, smooth and bare, looking like the impression of a cart wheel through the herbage.'"

"I am sorry the children have missed all this interesting information," said Violet.

"Never mind, my dear," said her husband. "It can be repeated to them tomorrow. I think there is a storm gathering, and that we are likely to have to stay at home here for a day or two."

"Should it prove a storm of any violence, we may be thankful that we are in this good, safe harbor," remarked Mr. Dinsmore.

"And that we have great abundance of good company and good reading matter," added Grandma Elsie.

"Yes," responded her father. "Those are truly additional causes for thankfulness."

"The little monkeys are another," laughed Lucilla. "I think we will have some fun with them, and certainly the children are delighted with their new pets."

"They certainly are engaging little monkeys—very different from those we are accustomed to see going about our streets with organ-grinders," said Grandma Dinsmore.

The children were on deck unusually early the next morning—their pets with them. They found their father, mother, Eva, and Lucilla there. The usual affectionate morning greetings were exchanged. Then, smiling down upon Elsie and her pet, the captain said, "I think you have not yet tired of your new pet, daughter?"

"No, indeed, papa," was the quick, earnest rejoinder. "I'm growing fonder of him every hour. Oh, he's just the dearest little fellow!"

"And so is mine," added Ned. "I think I'll name him 'Tee-tee.' As Elsie's is a little smaller than mine, she is going to call him 'Tiny'."

"If papa approves," added Elsie.

"I am well satisfied," returned their father. "You have begun your day earlier than usual," Captain Raymond went on, addressing the two children. "I am well pleased that it is so, because now you can take some exercise about the deck, which may be prevented later by a storm," and he glanced up at the sky where black clouds were quickly gathering.

"Yes, papa, we will," they answered, and they set off at once upon a race around the deck, carrying their pets with them.

The storm had begun when the summons to breakfast came, but the faces that gathered about the table were cheerful and bright. All agreed that it would be no hardship to have to remain on board for some days with plenty of books and periodicals to read, the plesant company which they were to each other, and the abundance of fruits and other dainties that the captain always provided for their enjoyment.

When they were finished eating, they repaired to the salon, held their usual morning service, and sat about singly or in small groups talking, reading, writing, or, if a lady, busied with some fancy work.

The children were much taken up with their new pets, petting them and letting them climb about on their shoulders.

Cousin Ronald watched them with interest and pleasure. Elsie was standing near with Tiny on her shoulder, who gazing into her eyes with a look that seemed to say, "You are so kind to me that I love you already." Elsie stroked and patted him, saying, "You dear little pet! I love you already and mean to take the best care of you."

"Thanks, dear little mistress. I am glad to belong to you and mean to be always the best little tee-tee that ever was seen." The words seemed to come from the tee-tee's lips, and its pretty eyes were looking right into Elsie's own.

"Why, you little dear!" she said with a pleased little laugh, stroking and patting him, then glancing round at Cousin Ronald, "How well you talk. In English, too, though I don't believe you ever heard the language before you came aboard the *Dolphin*."

"No, we didn't. Though we can speak it now as well as any other," Ned's pet seemed to say, lifting its head from his shoulder and glancing around at its brother.

That brought a merry laugh from its little master. "Speak English as much as you please, Tee-tee," he said, fondly stroking his pet's fur, "or talk Portuguese or any other language you're acquainted with."

"I'm afraid they will never be able to talk unless Cousin Ronald is in the company," said Elsie. "Or Brother Max," she added.

"Yes, Brother Max could make them talk just as well," said Ned. "Oh, here come the letters and papers!" as a sailor came in carrying the mailbag.

Its contents gave employment to everyone for a time, but, after a little, Violet, having finished the perusal of her share, called the children to her and gave them an interesting account of the talk of the night before about the strange doings of South American ants. They were much interested and asked a good many questions. When that subject was exhausted, Elsie asked to be told something about Rio de Janeiro.

"There is a maritime province of that name in the southeastern part of Brazil," her mother said.

"I have read that in the southern part of it, the scenery is very beautiful. The middle of the province is mountainous. About the city, I will read you from the New International Encyclopedia, which your father keeps on board whenever we are using the yacht."

She took down the book, opened it, and read: "'Rio de Janeiro, generally called Rio, the capital of the Brazillian empire, and the largest and most important commercial emporium of South America, stands on a magnificent harbor, seventy-five miles west of Cape Frio. The harbor or bay of Rio de Janeiro, is said, and apparently with justice, to be the most beautiful, secure, and spacious bay in the world, is land-locked, being entered from the south by a passage about a mile in width. It extends inland seventeen miles, and has an extreme breadth of about twelve miles. Of its numerous islands, the largest, Governor's Island, is six miles long. The entrance of the bay, guarded on either side by granite mountains, is deep, and is so safe that the harbor is made without the aid of pilots. On the left of the entrance rises the peak called, from its peculiar shape, Sugarloaf Mountain. All round the bay the blue waters are girdled with mountains and lofty hills of every variety of picturesque and fantastic outline. The harbor is protected by a number of fortresses. The city stands on the west shore of the bay, about four miles from its mouth. Seven green and mound-like hills diversify its sire; and the white-walled and vermillion-roofed houses cluster in the intervening valleys and climb the eminences in long lines. From the central portion of the city, lines of houses extend four miles in three principal directions. The old town, nearest the bay, is laid out in squares. The streets cross at right angles, are narrow, and are paved and flagged. The houses, often built of granite, are commonly two stories high. West of it is the elegantly-built new town, and the two districts are separated by the Campo de Santa Anna, an immense square or park on different parts of which stand an extensive garrison, the town hall, the national museum, the palace of the senate, the foreign office, and a large opera house. From a number of springs which rise on and around Mount Corcovado (three thousand feet high, and situated three and a half miles southwest of the city) water is conveyed to Rio de Janeiro by a splendid aqueduct and supplies the fountains with which the numerous squares are furnished. General municipal improvements have, within recent years, been introduced. Most of the streets are now as well paved as those of the finest European capitals. The city is abundantly lighted with gas, and commodious wharfs and quays are built along the water edge. Rio de Janeiro contains several excellent hospitals and infirmaries, asylums for foundlings and female orphans, other charitable institutions, some richly endowed, about fifty chapels and churches, generally costly and imposing structures with rich internal decorations, and several convents and nunneries. In the College of Pedro II, founded in 1837, the various branches of a liberal education are efficiently taught by a staff of eight or nine professors. The Imperial Academy of Medicine with a full corps of professors is attended by upward of three hundred students. There is also a theological seminary. The national library contains one-hundred thousand volumes.'

"There, my dears, I think that is all that will interest you," concluded Violet, closing the book.

CHAPTER FIFTEENTH

THE STORM CONTINUED for some days, during which the *Dolphin* lay quietly at anchor in the bay of Pará. It was a quiet, uneventful time for her passengers, but they enjoyed themselves well in each other's society and waited patiently for a change in the weather.

Finally it came. The sun shone, the waves had quieted down, and a gentle breeze had taken the place of the boisterous wind of the last few days.

Just as the sun rose, the anchor was lifted, and, to the joy of all on board, the yacht went on her way, steaming out of the harbor and then down the coast of Brazil. It was a long voyage, but, under the circumstances, by no means unpleasant to the *Dolphin's* passengers, so fond they were of each other's society.

At length they arrived at Rio de Janeiro. They stayed there long enough to acquaint themselves with its beauties and all that might interest a stranger and visitor.

All that accomplished, they left for the north, as it was getting near the time when even the invalids might safely return to the cooler climate of their home region.

It was evening. The children had retired for the night, and all the older ones were together on the deck. A silence that had lasted for some moments was broken by Lucilla. "You are taking us home now, I suppose, father?"

"I don't remember to have said so," replied the captain pleasantly. "Though very likely I may do so if you all wish it."

Then Violet spoke up in her quick, lively way, "Mamma, if you would give us all an invitation to visit Viamede, I think it would be delightful to go there for a week or two. Then Chester could see his sisters and their children."

"I should be glad to help him do so and very glad to have you all as my guests at Viamede," was the reply in Grandma Elsie's sweet tones.

Then came a chorus of thanks for her kind invitation. All seemed pleased with the idea.

"It will be quite a journey," remarked Lucilla in a tone of satisfaction.

"You are not weary of life on shipboard, daughter?" her father queried with a pleased, little laugh.

"No, indeed, father. I am very fond of life on the *Dolphin*. I suppose that is because of the sailor blood in me inherited from you."

"Some of which I have also," said Gracie. "I dearly love a voyage in the *Dolphin*."

"Which some of the rest of us do, too, without having the excuse of inherited sailor blood," said Harold with a wide grin.

"No. That inheritance isn't at all necessary to the enjoyment of life on the *Dolphin*," remarked Chester in his pleasant way.

"Indeed, it is not," said Evelyn. "I am certainly a landsman's daughter, but life on this vessel with the dear friends always to be found on it is delightful to me."

"And the rest of us can give a like testimony," said Mrs. Lilburn, and those who had not already spoken gave a hearty assent.

"Up this South American coast, through the Caribbean Sea and the Gulf of Mexico — it will be quite a voyage," remarked Lucilla, reflectively. "It is well, indeed, that we are all fond of life on the *Dolphin*."

"Yes. You will have had a great deal of it by the time we get home," said her father.

"Tomorrow is Sunday," remarked Grandma Elsie. "I am very glad we can have services on board. I often find them quite as helpful as those I attend on shore."

"Yes. I don't know why we shouldn't have services, though there is no licensed preacher among us," said the captain. "Certainly, we may all read God's Word, talk of it to others, and address to Him both prayers and praises."

The next morning after breakfast, all assembled upon deck and united in prayer and praise. The captain read a sermon, and then Mr. Lilburn, by request of the others, led them in their usual Bible lesson.

"Let us take the thirteenth and fourteenth chapters of Numbers for our lesson today," he said, reading the passage aloud. Then he asked, "Can you tell me, Cousin Elsie, where the children if Israel were encamped at this time?"

"At Kadesh, in what is called the wilderness of Paran. It was at a little distance to the southern end of the Dead Sea."

"They went and searched the land, as Moses directed, and cut down and brought back with them a cluster of grapes. A very large one, it must have been, for they bore it between two men upon a staff. They also brought pomegranates and figs. Do you know, Neddie, what *Eshcol* means?" asked Cousin Ronald.

"No, sir. Papa hasn't taught me that yet," replied the little boy.

"It means a bunch of grapes," said Cousin Ronald, smiling kindly on the little fellow. "Gracie, do you think the spies were truthful?"

"They seem to have been, so far as the facts about the country they had just visited were concerned," Gracie answered. Then she read, "'And they told him, and said, "We came unto the land whither thou sendest us, and surely it floweth with milk and honey; and this is the fruit of it. Nevertheless, the people be strong that dwell in the land, and the cities are walled, and very great: and, moreover, we saw the children of Anak there. The Amalekites dwell in the land of the south: and the Hitties, and the Jebusites . . . and the Canaanites dwell by the sea, and by the coast of Jordan."'"

"Truly, a very discouraging report," said Mr. Lilburn. "For though they described the land as very good and desirable, they evidently considered its inhabitants too strong to be overcome."

He then read, "'And they brought up an evil report of the land which they had searched unto the children of Israel, saying, "The land, through which we have gone to search it, is a land that eateth up the inhabitants thereof; and all the people that we saw in it are men of a great stature. And there we saw giants: and we were in our own sight as grasshoppers, and so we were in their sight."' And what effect had their report upon the people, Cousin Violet?" he asked.

In reply, Violet read, "'And all the congregation lifted up their voice, and cried; and the people wept that night. And all the children of Israel murmured against Moses and against Aaron: and the whole congregation said unto them, "Would God that we had died in the land of Egypt! Or would God we had died in the wilderness! And wherefore hath the Lord brought us unto this land, to fall by the sword, that our wives and our children should be a prey? Were it not better for us to return into Egypt?" And they said one to another, "Let us make a captain, and let us return into Egypt."'"

It seemed to be Mr. Dinsmore's turn, and he read, "'And Joshua the son of Nun; and Caleb the son of Jephunneh, which were of them that searched the land, rent their clothes: And they spake unto all the company of the children of

Israel, saying, "The land, which we passed through to search it, is exceeding good land. If the Lord delight in us, then He will bring us into this land, and give it us; a land which floweth with milk and honey. Only rebel not ye against the Lord, neither fear ye the people of the land; for they are bread for us: their defense is departed from them, and the Lord is with us: fear them not."'"

Then Mrs. Dinsmore read, "'But all the congregation bade stone them with stones. And the glory of the Lord appeared in the tabernacle of the congregation before all the children of Israel. And the Lord said unto Moses, "How long will this people provoke Me? And how long will it be ere they believe me, for all the signs which I have shewed among them? I will smite them with the pestilence, and disinherit them, and will make thee a greater nation and mightier than they."'"

"How very childish they were," remarked Violet. "Why should they wish they had died in the land of Egypt, or in the wilderness? That would have been no better than dying where they were. And it does seem strange they could not trust in God when He had given them such wonderful deliverances."

"'And they said, one to another, "Let us make a captain, and let us return into Egypt,"'" read Harold. Then, he added, "It does seem as though they felt Moses would not do anything so wicked and foolish as going back into Egypt."

"And they might well feel so," said the captain. "Moses was not the man to be discouraged by such difficulties after all the wonders God had shown him and them in Egypt and on their way the wilderness."

"That is true," said Mr. Lilburn. "But let us go on to the end of the story. We have read that the Lord threatened to smite them with the pestilence, disinherit them, and make of Moses a greater nation mightier than they. Chester, what did Moses say in reply?"

"'And Moses said unto the Lord, "Then the Egyptians shall hear it (for Thou broughtest up this people in Thy might from among them;) and they will tell it to the inhabitants of this land: for they have heard . . . that Thou Lord art seen face to face, and that Thy cloud standeth over them, and that Thou goest before them, by day time in the pillar of a cloud, and in a pillar of fire by night. Now if Thou shalt kill all this people as one man, then the nations which have heard the fame of Thee will speak, saying, 'Because the Lord was not able to bring this people into the land which He sware unto them, therefore He hath slain them in the wilderness.' And now, I beseech Thee, let the power of my Lord be great, according as Thou hast spoken, saying, 'The Lord is long suffering, and of great mercy, forgiving iniquity and transgression, and by no means clearing the guilty, visiting the iniquity of the fathers upon the children unto the third and fourth generation.' Pardon, I beseech Thee, the iniquity of this people according unto the greatness of Thy mercy, and as Thou hast forgiven this people, from Egypt even until now.'"

Chester paused, and Mrs. Dinsmore took up the story where he dropped it, reading from her Bible, "'And the Lord said, "I have pardoned according to thy word: But as truly as I live, all the earth shall be filled with the glory of the Lord. Because all those men which have seen My glory, and My miracles, which I did in Egypt and in the wilderness, and have tempted Me now these ten times, and have not hearkened to My voice; Surely they shall not see the land which I sware unto their fathers, neither shall any of them that provoked Me see it: But My servant Caleb, because he had another spirit with him, and hath followed Me fully, him will I bring into the land whereinto he went; and his seed shall possess it. (Now the Amalekites and the Canaanites dwelt in the valley.) Tomorrow turn you, and get you into the wilderness by . . . the Red Sea."'"

"Papa, did all those people lose their souls?" asked Elsie.

"I hope not," he replied. "If they repented, they were forgiven and reached Heaven at last. Jesus says, 'Come unto Me, all ye that labour and are heavy laden, and I will give you rest. Take My yoke upon you and learn of Me; for I am meek and lowly in heart: and ye shall find rest unto your souls.'"

CHAPTER SIXTEENTH

"ARE WE GOING TO stop at any of these South American countries, papa?" asked Elsie the next day, standing by her father's side on the deck.

"I hardly think so," he replied. "It is too nearly time to go home."

"Oh, papa, I'd like ever so much to see our other home, Viamede. Grandma lets me call it one of my homes. If there is time, and it isn't too far away."

"Well, daughter," her father said with a smile, "I think there is time, and the place not too far away, the *Dolphin* being a good-natured yacht that never complains of her long journeys."

"Oh, papa, are we really going there?" cried the little girl, fairly dancing with delight. "I'll be so glad to see the Keith cousins at the cottage, and those at Magnolia Hall, and the others at Torriswood. And I'll show Tiny to them, and they'll be sure to be pleased to see him," she added, hugging her pet, which, as usual, she had in her arms."

"Probably they will," said her father. "Do you think you'll give him to any one of them?"

"Give my little pet Tiny away? Why, papa! No, indeed! I couldn't even think of such a thing!" she cried, hugging her pet closer. "I'm fond of him, papa, and I'm pretty sure he's fond of me. He seems to want to snuggle up close to me all the time."

"Yes, I think he is fond of you and won't want to leave you, except for a little while now and then to run up and down the trees and around the grounds. That will be his play, and when he gets hungry, he will go back to you for something to eat."

Ned, with his pet in his arms, had joined them just in time to hear his father's last sentence.

"Are you speaking about Elsie's Tiny, papa?" he asked.

"Yes, my son, and what I said will apply to your Tee-tee just as well. I think if my children are good and kind to the little fellows, they will not want to run away."

"I have been good to him so far," said Ned, patting and stroking his pet as he spoke. "I mean to keep on. Papa, where are we going now? Elsie and I were talking about it a while ago, and we wondered if we were now on our way home."

"Would you like to be?" asked his father.

"Yes, papa, or to go somewhere else first—just as it pleases you."

"What would you say to visiting Viamede?"

"Oh, papa, that I'd like it ever so much!"

"Well, your grandma has given us all an invitation to go there, and we are very likely to accept it. It will make us a little later getting home than I had intended, but it will be so great a pleasure that I think we will all feel paid."

"Yes, indeed!" cried Ned, dancing up and down in delight. "I think it's just splendid that we can go there. I don't know any lovelier or more delightful place to go to. Do you, papa?"

"And I'm as glad as you are, Ned," said Elsie. "Let's go and thank grandma. Yonder she is in her usual seat under the awning."

"Yes," said their father, "you owe her thanks, and it would be well to give it at once." They hastened to do his bidding.

Grandma Elsie was seated with the other ladies of their party in that pleasant spot under the awning, where there were plenty of comfortable seats and they were protected from sun and shower. The gentlemen were there, too. Some were reading and some—the younger ones—were chatting and laughing merrily among themselves. Into this group the children came rushing, full of excitement and glee.

"Oh, grandma," they cried, talking both at once, "we're so glad we're going to Viamede. We're so much obliged to you for inviting us, because it's such a dear, beautiful place and seems to be one of our homes."

"Yes, you must always consider it so, my dear, little grandchildren. Because Viamede is mine and I consider my dear grandchildren as mine, too," was Grandma Elsie's smiling and affectionate rejoinder.

"As I do, mamma," said Violet. "I am sure no children ever had a better, kinder grandmother."

"No, indeed," said Elsie. "And I think Tiny and Tee-tee will enjoy being at Viamede, too, and climbing up the beautiful trees. Papa says they will but will be glad to come back to us when they get hungry. Because we feed them with such things as they like to eat."

"It will be a long journey before we get to Viamede. Won't it, mamma?" asked Ned.

"Yes, a good many miles up this coast of South America then through the Caribbean Sea and the Gulf of Mexico to New Orleans. Then we will go through Teche Bayou to Viamede. I think it will be a long but pleasant journey. Don't you?"

"Yes, mamma, it is very pleasant to be on our yacht with you and papa and our sisters and grandma and so many other kind friends."

Just then the captain joined them.

"How long will it take us to get to Viamede, papa?" asked Ned.

"About as long as it would to cross the ocean from our country to Europe. And should storms compel us to seek refuge for a time in some harbor, it will, of course, take longer."

"Will we go back to Trinidad?"

"Hardly, I think. Though we will probably pass in sight of the island."

"And we are on the coast of Brazil now?"

"Yes, and we will be for a week or more."

"We are trying life in the *Dolphin* for a good while this winter," said Violet.

"You are not wearying of it, I hope, my dear?" asked the captain, giving her a rather anxious and troubled look.

"Oh, no, not at all!" she replied, giving him an affectionate smile. "This winter trip has been a real enjoyment to me thus far."

"As it has to all of us, I think," said her mother. All within hearing joined in with their expressions of pleasure in all they had experienced on the sea or on the land since sailing away from their homes in the *Dolphin*.

"I am half afraid that you gentlemen will find your homes but dull places when you get back to them," remarked Lucilla in a tone of feigned melancholy, sighing deeply as she spoke.

"Well, for business reasons I shall be glad to get back to my office," said Chester. "So it will not be altogether a trying thing to return, even if my home is to be but dull and wearisome," he continued, teasing his wife in return.

"I don't believe it will be," laughed Gracie. "Lu is never half so hard and disagreeable as she pretends. She has always been the nicest of sisters to me, and I have an idea that she is quite as good as a wife."

"So have I," said Chester. "I know I wouldn't swap wives with any man."

"Nor I husbands with any woman," laughed Lucilla. "I took this man for better or for worse, but there's no worse about it."

A merry laugh from little Elsie turned all eyes upon her. Tiny was curled up on her shoulder, his hazel eyes fixed inquiringly upon her face and one of his fingers gently laid upon her lips.

"I think Tiny wants to learn to talk," her father said. "He seems to be trying to see how it is you do it."

"Oh, do you think he can learn, papa?" she asked in eager tones. "I don't see why monkeys shouldn't talk as well as parrots."

"I do not, either, my child. I only know that they do not."

At that instant, Tiny lifted his head and turned his eyes upon the captain, and some words seemed to come rapidly and in rather an indignant tone from his lips. "I can talk, and I will when I want to. My little mistress is very kind and good to me, and I'm growing very fond of her."

Everybody laughed, and Elsie said, "I wish it were really his talk. But I know it was Cousin Ronald who spoke."

"Ah, little cousin, how much fun you miss by knowing too much," laughed Mr. Lilburn.

Then Ned's Tee-tee seemed to speak. "You needn't make all that fuss over my brother. I can talk quite as well as he can."

"Why, so you can!" exclaimed Ned, stroking and patting him. "And I'm as glad as I can say to have you talk just as much as you will, my little pet, Tee-tee."

"Thank you, little master. You're very good to me," was the reply.

"Now, Tiny, it is your turn," said Elsie to her pet. "I hope you think you are having a good time here on this yacht?"

"Yes, indeed I do," was the reply. "But where are we going?"

"To Viamede, a beautiful place in Louisiana. And you shall run about over the velvety, flower-spangled lawn and climb the trees, if you want to. You can pick some oranges and bananas for yourself and have such a good time."

"That's nice! Shall my brother Tee-tee have a good time with me, too?"

"Yes, if you both promise not to run away and leave us."

"We'd be very foolish tee-tees if we did."

"So I think," laughed Elsie, affectionately stroking and patting Tiny.

"Come, Tee-tee. It's your turn to talk a little," said Ned, petting his monkey.

"Am I going to that good place Tiny's mistress tells about, where they have fine trees to climb and oranges and bananas and other good things to eat?" Tee-tee seemed to ask.

"Yes," replied Ned. "If you keep on being a good fellow, you shall go there and have a good time playing about and feasting on the fruits, nuts, and other nice things."

"Then I mean to be good—as good as I know how, my little master."

"Cousin Ronald, you do make them talk very nicely," remarked Elsie with obvious satisfaction,

Then she added, "But I really do wish they could do it themselves."

"I presume they would be glad if they could," said Lucilla. "Yours watches the movements of your lips, as if he wanted very much to imitate them with his."

"And I believe he does," said Elsie. "It makes me feel more thankful for the gift of speech than I ever was before."

"Then it has a good effect," said her father.

"So they are useful little creatures, after all," said Gracie. "I had thought of them only as little playthings, papa."

"I think Tiny is the very best plaything that I ever had," said Elsie, again stroking and patting the little fellow. "Cousin Ronald, won't you please make him talk a little more?"

"Why do you want me to talk so much, little mistress?" Tiny seemed to ask.

"Oh, because I like to hear you, and you really mean what you seem to say. Do you like to be with us on this nice big yacht?"

"Pretty well, though I'd rather be among the big trees in the woods where I was born."

"I think that must be because you are not quite civilized," laughed Elsie.

"I'd rather be in those woods, too" Tee-tee seemed to say. "Let's run away to the woods, Tiny, when we get a chance."

"Ho, ho!" cried Ned. "If that's the way you talk, you shan't have a chance."

"Now, Ned, you surely wouldn't be so cruel as to keep him if he wants to go back to his native woods," said Lucilla. "How would you like to be carried off to a strange place away from papa and mamma?"

"But I ain't a monkey," said Ned. "And I don't believe he cares about his father and mother as I do about mine. Do you care very much about them, Tee-tee?"

"Not so very much, and I think they've been caught or killed."

The words seemed to come from Tee-tee's lips, and Ned exclaimed triumphantly, "There! He doesn't care a bit."

"But it was not he that answered, Ned. It was Cousin Ronald."

"Well, maybe Cousin Ronald knows how he feels. Don't you, Cousin Ronald?"

"Ah, I must acknowledge that it is all guess work, sonny boy," laughed the old gentleman.

"Well," said Ned reflectively, "I've heard there are some folks who are good at guessing, and I believe you are one of them, Cousin Ronald. But I'm not a Yankee, you know, and I've heard that they are the folks who are good at guessing. I think other folks must do some of it," said Ned.

"Quite likely," said Cousin Ronald. "Most folks like to engage in that business once in awhile."

"Tee-tee," said Ned, "I wish you and Tiny would talk a little more."

"What about, little master?" seemed to come in quick response from Tiny's lips.

"Oh, anything you please. All I want is the fun of hearing you talk," said Ned.

"It wouldn't be polite for us to do all the talking," he seemed to respond.

Ned returned, "You needn't mind about the politeness of it. We folks all want to hear you talk, whatever you may say."

"But I don't want to talk unless I actually have something to say," was Tiny's answer.

"That's right, Tiny. You seem to be a sensible fellow," laughed Lucilla.

"Papa, are monkeys mischievous animals?" asked Elsie.

"They have that reputation, and certainly some have shown themselves so. Therefore, you had better not put temptation in the way of Tiny or Tee-tee."

"And better not trust them too far," said Violet. "I'd be sorry to have any of your clothes torn up while we are so far from home."

"Oh, mamma, do you think they would do that?" cried Elsie.

"I don't know, but I have heard of monkeys meddling with their mistress's clothes. Perhaps Tiny doesn't know how much too large yours would be for her—no for him."

"Well, mamma, I'll try to keep things out of his way, and I hope he'll realize that a girl's garments are not suitable for a boy monkey," laughed Elsie. "Do you hear that? And will you remember it, little man?" she asked, giving him a little shake and tap that he seemed to take very unconcernedly.

"And I'll try to keep my clothes out of Tee-tee's way. I shouldn't like to make trouble for you, mamma, or to wear either holey or patched clothes," said Ned.

"No," said his father. "So we will hope the little fellows will be honest enough to refrain from meddling with your clothes, at least till we get home, Ned."

"And I think you will find these pretty little fellows honest and not meddlesome," said Mr. Dinsmore. "I have read that they are most engaging little creatures, and from what I have seen of these, I think that is true;. They seem to behave with gentle intelligence quite superior to that of any other monkey I ever saw and to have amiable tempers, too, and there is an innocent expression in their countenances, which is very pleasing. I do not think they have as yet had anything to frighten them here, but I have read that when alarmed, sudden tears fill their clear hazel eyes, and they make little imploring, shrinking gestures that excite the sympathy of those to whom they are appealing for protection."

"Yes, grandpa, I think they do look good— better and more pleasant than any other monkey that I ever saw," said Ned.

"Yes," said his father, "it is certainly the most engaging specimen of the monkey family that I ever came across."

"Children," said Violet, "the call to dinner will come in about five minutes. So put away your pets for the present and make yourselves neat for the table."

CHAPTER
SEVENTEENTH

THE *DOLPHIN* SPED on her way, and her passengers enjoyed their voyage whether the sun shone or the decks were swept by wind and rain, for the salon was always a comfortable place of refuge in stormy weather and by no means an unpleasant one at any time. They were all gathered on the deck one bright, breezy morning chatting cheerily, the children amusing themselves with their tee-tee pets.

"Father," said Lucilla, "are we not nearing the Caribbean Sea?"

"Yes. If all goes well, we will be in it by this time tomorrow," was Captain Raymond's reply. "It is a body of water worth seeing—separated from the Gulf of Mexico by Yucatan, and from the Atlantic Ocean by the great arch of the Antilles between Cuba and Trinidad. It forms the turning point in the vast cycle of waters known as the Gulf Stream that wheels round regularly from Southern Africa to Northern Europe. The Caribbean Sea pours its waters into the Gulf of Mexico on the west, which shoots forth east of the Florida stream with the computed volume of three thousand Mississippis."

"But, papa, where does it get so much water to pour out?" asked Elsie. "I wonder it didn't get empty long ago."

"Ah, that is prevented by its taking in as well as pouring out. It gathers water from the Atlantic Ocean and the Amazon and Orinoco Rivers."

"Papa, why do they call it by that name—Caribbean Sea?" asked Ned.

"It takes its name from the Caribs, the people who were living on the islands when Columbus discovered them," said the captain.

"The Gulf Stream is very important. Isn't it, papa?" asked Elsie.

"The most important and best known of the great ocean currents," he replied. "It flows out of the Gulf of Mexico, between the coast of Florida on one side and the Cuba and Bahama islands and shoals on the other."

"The Stream is very broad, isn't it, papa?" asked Gracie.

"About fifty miles in the narrowest portion, and it has a velocity of five miles an hour, pouring along like an immense torrent."

"But where does it run to, papa?" asked Ned.

"First in a northeasterly direction, along the American coast, the current gradually growing wider and less swift until it reaches the island and banks of Newfoundland. Then it sweeps across the Atlantic and divides into two portions, one tuning eastward toward the Azores and coast of Morocco, while the other laps the shores of the British islands, Norway, and the southern borders of Iceland and Spitzbergen, nearly as far east as Nova Zembla."

"But how can they tell where it goes when it mixes in with other waters, papa?" asked Elsie.

"Its waters are of a deep indigo blue, while those of the sea are light green," replied her father. "And as it pours out of the Gulf of Mexico, its waters are very warm and full of fish and seaweed in great masses. Its waters are so warm that in mid-winter, off the cold coasts of America between Cape Hatteras and Newfoundland, ships beaten back from their harbors by fierce northwesters until loaded down with ice and in danger of foundering turn their prows to the east and seek relief and comfort in the Gulf Stream."

"Don't they have some difficulty in finding it, father?" asked Lucilla.

"A bank of fog rising like a wall, caused by the condensation of warm vapors meeting a colder atmosphere, marks the edge of the stream," replied the captain. "Also the water suddenly changes from green to blue, the climate from winter to summer, and this change is so sudden that when a ship is crossing the line, a difference of thirty degrees of temperature has been marked between the bow and the stern."

"Papa, I know there used to be pirates in the West Indies. Was it there that Kidd committed his crimes?"

"I think not," replied her father. "In his day, piracy on the high seas prevailed to an alarming extent, especially in the Indian Ocean. It was said that many of the freebooters came from America, and that they found a ready market here for their stolen goods. The King of England — then King of this country, also — wished to put an end to piracy and instructed the governors of New York and Massachusetts to put down these abuses.

"It was soon known in New York that the new governor was bent on suppressing piracy. Then some men of influence, who knew Kidd as a successful, bold, and skillful captain, who had fought against the French and performed some daring exploits, recommended him as commander of the expedition against the pirates. They said he had all the requisite qualifications — skill, courage, large and widely-extended naval experience, and thorough knowledge of the haunts of the pirates 'who prowled between the Cape of Good Hope and the Straits of Malacca.'

"A private company was organized, and a vessel bought. It was called the *Adventure* and was equipped with thirty guns, and Kidd was given command. He sailed to New York, and on his way, he captured a French ship off the coast of Newfoundland. He sailed from the Hudson River in January, 1697, crossed the ocean, and reached the coast of Madagascar — then the great rendezvous point of the buccaneers."

"And how soon did he begin his piracy, papa?"

"I can't tell you exactly, but it soon began to be reported that he was doing so. In November, 1698, orders were sent to all governors of English colonies to apprehend him if he came within their jurisdiction.

"In April of 1699, he arrived in the West Indies in a vessel called *Quidah Merchant*, secured her in a lagoon on the Island of Samoa southeast of Haiti, and then, in a sloop called *San Antonio*, sailed for the north, up the coast into Delaware Bay, afterward to Long Island Sound, and into Oyster Bay. He was soon arrested, charged with piracy, sent to England, tried, found guilty, and hung."

"There were other charges. Were there not, captain?" asked Mr. Dinsmore.

"Yes, sir—there were charges of burning houses, massacring peasantry, brutally treating prisoners, and particularly murdering one of his men, William Moore. He had called Moore a dog, to which Moore replied, 'Yes, I am a dog, but it is you that have made me so.' At that, Kidd, in a fury of rage, struck him down with a bucket, killing him instantly. It was found impossible to prove piracy against Kidd, but he was found guilty of the murder of Moore, and on the twenty-fourth of May, 1701, he was hanged with nine of his accomplices."

"Did he own that he was guilty, papa?"

"No," replied the captain, "he protested his innocence to the last. He said he had been coerced by his men and that Moore had been mutinous when he struck him. There are many who think his trial was high-handed and unfair."

"Then I hope he didn't deserve quite all that has been said against him," said Gracie.

"I hope not," said her father.

CHAPTER
EIGHTEENTH

ELSIE AND NED WERE on the deck with their tee-tees, which seemed to be in a more than usually playful mood, running round and round the deck and up and down the masts. Ned chased after them, trying to catch them, but he failed again and again. He grew more and more excited and less careful to avoid mishap in the struggle to capture the little runaways. Elsie called after him to "let them have their fun for awhile, and then they would come back to be petted and fed," but he paid no attention to her. He called and whistled to Tee-tee, who was high up on the mast. The little fellow stood still for a time, regarding his young master as if he would say, "I'll come when I please, but you can't make me come sooner." So Ned read the look and called up to him, "Come down this minute, you little rascal, or I'll be apt to make you sorry you didn't."

That did not seem to have any effect, and Ned looked about for someone to send up after the little runaway.

"Have patience, master Ned. He'll come down after a bit," said a sailor standing near. "Ah, do you see? There he comes now," and turning quickly, Ned saw his tee-tee running swiftly down the mast, then along the top of the gunwale, then down on the outside. He rushed to catch him, leaned too far over, and, with a cry of terror, felt himself falling down, down into the sea.

A scream from Elsie echoed his cry. The sailor who had spoken to Ned a moment before instantly tore off his coat and plunged in after the child, caught him as he rose to the surface, held his head out of the water, and called for a boat, which was already being launched by the other sailors.

Neither the captain nor any of his older passengers were on deck at the moment, but the cries of the children, the sailor's plunge into the water, and the hurrying of the others to launch the boat were heard in the salon.

"Something is wrong!" exclaimed the captain, hurrying to the deck closely followed by Violet.

"Oh, my children! What has happened to them?" was her cry.

The other members of the party came hurrying after them all in great excitement.

"Don't be alarmed, my dear," said the captain, soothingly. "Whatever is wrong can doubtless be set right in a few moments." Then, catching sight of his little girl as he gained the deck and seeing that she was crying bitterly, "Elsie, daughter, what is it?" he asked.

"Oh, papa," sobbed the child, "Neddie has fallen into the sea, and I'm afraid he's drowned!"

Before her father could answer, a sailor approached and, bowing respectfully, said, "I think it will be all right, sir, in a few minutes. Master Ned fell into the water, but Tom Jones happened to be close at hand and sprang in right after him and caught him as he came up the first time. Then he called to us to lower the boat, and you see it's in the water already, and they're starting after Master Ned and Tom who have been left considerably behind now by the forward movement of the yacht."

"Ah, yes. I see them," returned the captain, "the boat, too. Violet, my dear, Neddie seems to be quite safe, and we will have him on board again in a few minutes."

All on the deck watched in almost breathless suspense the progress of the small boat through the water. They saw it reach and pick up the half-drowning man and boy and then return to the yacht. In a few moments more, Ned was in his mother's arms, her tears falling on his face, as she clasped him to herself, kissing him over and over again with passionate fondness.

"There, Vi, dear, you had better give him into my care for a little while," said Harold. "He wants a good rubbing, dry garments, a dose of something hot, and then a good nap."

"There, go with Uncle Harold, dear," said his mother, releasing him.

"And papa, too," said Ned, looking up at his father entreatingly.

"Yes, little son, papa will go with you," returned the captain in moved tones.

"Oh, is my tee-tee drowned?" exclaimed the little fellow with sudden recollection, glancing around as he spoke.

"No," said Harold. "I see him now running around the deck. He's all right." With that, the two gentlemen hurried down into the cabin, taking Ned with them.

"Well, it is a very good plan to always take a doctor along when we go sailing about the world," remarked Lucilla, looking after them as they passed down the stairway.

"Yes, especially when you can find one as skillful, kind, and agreeable as our Doctor Harold," said Evelyn.

"Thank you, my dear," said Mrs. Travilla, regarding Evelyn with a pleased smile. "He seems to me both an excellent physician and a polished gentleman, but mothers are apt to be partial judges. So I am glad to find that your opinion is much the same as mine."

Gracie looked gratified, and Violet said, "It seems to be the opinion of all on board."

"Mine as well as the rest," added Lucilla. "Chester has improved wonderfully since we set sail on the *Dolphin*."

"Quite true," said Chester's voice close at hand, he having just returned from a talk with the sailors who had picked up the half drowning man and boy, "quite true, and I give credit to my doctor, Cousin Harold—for his advice at least, which I have endeavored to follow carefully. He's a fine, competent physician, even if it is a relative who says it. Violet, you need have no fear that he won't bring your boy through this thing all right."

"I am not at all afraid to trust him—my dear, skillful brother and physician—and I believe he will be able to bring my little son through this trouble," said Violet.

"No doubt of it," returned Chester. "Tomorrow morning little Ned will be in usual health and spirits—none the worse for his sudden sea bath."

"I can never be thankful enough to Tom Jones," said Violet with emotion. "He saved the life of my darling boy. He surely would have drowned before anyone else could have reached him."

"Yes," said Chester. "I think he deserves all the praise you can give him."

"And something more than praise," said Violet and her mother, both speaking at once. "He is not, by any means, a rich man," added Violet. "My husband will certainly find a way to help him into better circumstances."

"Something in which I shall be glad to assist," added her mother. "Neddie is your son, but he is my dear little grandson."

"And my great-grandson," added Mr. Dinsmore, joining the group. "I am truly thankful that Tom Jones was so near when he fell and so ready to go to the rescue."

"As well as the engineer to slacken the speed of the vessel, and the other sailors to lower and man the boat and go to the rescue," added Violet.

"Yes. They must all be rewarded," said her mother. "It will be a pleasure to me to give them a substantial evidence of the gratitude I feel."

"That is just like you, mamma," said Violet with emotion. "But I am sure his father is more than able and will be more than willing to do all that is necessary."

"Yes, indeed!" exclaimed Lucilla. "There is no more just or generous person than my father! And he is abundantly able to do all that can be desired to reward any or all who took part in the saving of my dear, little brother."

"My dear girl," said Grandma Elsie, "no one who knows your father can have the least doubt of his generosity and kindness of heart. I am very sure that all the men we were speaking of will have abundant proof of it."

"As we all are," said Mr. Dinsmore.

"I'm sure papa will do just what is right. He always does," said little Elsie. "And oh, mamma, don't you think that he and Uncle Harold will soon get dear Neddie well of his dreadful dip in the sea?"

"I do, daughter," answered Violet. "Oh, here come your father and uncle now!"

At that moment, the two gentlemen stepped upon the deck and came swiftly toward them.

"Oh, how is he—my darling little son?" cried Violet, who was almost breathless with both excitement and anxiety.

"Doing as well as possible," answered her brother in cheery tones. "He has had a good rubbing down, a hot, soothing potion, been covered up in his berth, and fallen into a sound sleep."

"Yes," said the captain. "I think he is doing as well as possible, and tomorrow will show him no worse for his involuntary dip in the sea."

"Oh, I am so glad, so thankful!" exclaimed Violet, tears of joy filling her eyes.

"As I am," said his father, his voice trembling with emotion. "We have great cause for thankfulness to the Giver of all good. I am very glad your mind is relieved, dearest. But I must go now and thank the men, whose prompt action saved us from a heavy loss and a bitter sorrow."

He had seated himself by Violet's side and put his arm about her, but he rose with those last words and went forward to where a group of sailors were talking over the episode and rejoicing that it had ended so satisfactorily. They lifted their hats and saluted the captain respectfully as he neared them.

"How is the little lad, sir?" asked Jones, as he neared them. "No worse for his ducking, I hope."

"Thank you, Jones. I think he will not be any worse by tomorrow morning," replied the captain. "He is sleeping now, which, I think, is the best thing he could do. Jones, he owes his life to you, and I can never cease to be grateful to you for your prompt action in springing instantly to his rescue when he fell into the water."

"Oh, sir," stammered Jones, looking both pleased and embarrassed. "It—it wasn't a bit more than almost any other fellow would have done in my place. And I'm mighty glad I did it, for he's one o' the likeliest little chaps ever I saw!"

"He is a very dear one to both his father and mother, brother and sisters, and I should like to give to each of you fellows who helped in this thing some little token of my appreciation of your kindly efforts. I will think it over and have a talk with you again, and you may consider what return I should make that would be the most agreeable and helpful to you."

"About how much do you suppose that means?" asked one man of his mates, when the captain had walked away.

"Perhaps five dollars apiece," chuckled one of the others, "for the captain is pretty generous. Likely Jones's share will be twice as much."

"Nonsense! Who wants to be paid for saving that cute little chap from drowning?" growled Jones. "I'd have been a coward if I'd indulged in a minute's hesitation."

"I s'pose so," returned one of the others, "but you risked your life to save his. So, you deserve a big reward, and I hope and believe you'll get it."

On leaving the sailors, the captain went to the pilothouse and gave warm thanks there for the prompt slowing of the *Dolphin's* speed the instant the alarm of Ned's fall was given.

"It was no more than any other man would have done in my place, captain," replied the pilot with a smile of gratification.

"No," returned Captain Raymond, "some men would have been less prompt, and the probable consequence may have been the loss of my little son's life, which would have been a great loss to his mother and me," he added with emotion. "I think you are worthy of an increase of pay, Mr. Clark, and you won't object to it, I suppose?"

"No, sir. Seeing I have a family to support, I won't refuse your kindness, and I thank you very much for the kind offer."

At that moment, Violet drew near and stood at her husband's side. She spoke in tones trembling with emotion. "I have come to thank you, Mr. Clark, for the saving of my darling boy's life. I know that but for the slowing of the engine, both Jones and he might have lost their lives — sinking before help could reach them."

"You are very kind to look at it in that way, Mrs. Raymond," returned Clark in tones that spoke his appreciation of her grateful feeling. "But it was very little that I did — cost hardly any exertion and no risk. Jones is, I think, the only one deserving of much, if any, credit for the rescue of the little lad."

He paused a moment then added, "But the captain here has most generously offered me an increase of pay, for which I thank him most heartily."

"Oh, my dear, I am very glad to hear that!" exclaimed Violet, addressing her husband.

With the last word, her hand was slipped into his arm, and, with a parting nod to Clark, they turned and went back to the family group still gathered upon the deck under the awning.

They found Elsie with Tiny on her shoulder and Tee-tee on her lap.

"I must take care of them both now for till Ned gets over that dreadful sea bath," she said, looking up at her parents as they drew near.

"Yes, daughter, that is right," replied her father. "It is no fault of little Tee-tee that his young master fell into the sea."

That evening, Violet and the captain had a quiet promenade on the deck together, in which they talked of those who had any share in the rescue of their little Ned and what reward might be appropriate for each one.

"I have heard there is a mortgage on the farm that is home to Tom Jones and his mother," said the captain. "I will pay that off as a gift to Tom in recognition of his bravery and kindness in risking his own life in the effort to save that of our little son."

"Do," said Violet, joyfully. "He most certainly deserves it, and probably there is nothing he would like better."

"He is certainly entitled to the largest reward I can give," said the captain. "Though I daresay almost any of the others would have acted just as he did, if they had had the same opportunity."

Ned slept well under his uncle's care that night, and the next morning he appeared at the breakfast table, looking much as usual and saying in answer to loving inquiries that he felt as if nothing had happened to him—not a bit the worse for his bath in the sea.

Nor was he disposed to blame Tee-tee for his involuntary plunge into the water. The two were evidently as fast friends as ever.

After breakfast, the captain had a talk, first with Jones, then with the other men, in which each learned what his reward was to be. Jones was almost too much moved for speech when told of his, but he expressed his gratitude more fully afterward, saying, "It is a blessed thing to have a home of one's own, especially when it can be shared with one's mother. Dear me, but won't she be glad!"

And the others were highly pleased with the ten dollars apiece that fell to their share.

CHAPTER
NINETEENTH

THE YACHT HAD NOW passed from the Caribbean Sea into the Gulf of Mexico and was headed for New Orleans, where they arrived safely and in due season.

They did not care to visit the city—most of them having been there several times. All wanted to spend at Viamede the few days they could spare for rest and pleasure before returning to their more northern homes. So they tarried but a few hours at the Crescent City then pursued their way along the gulf, up the bay into Teche Bayou, and beyond through lake and lakelet, past plantation and swamp, plain and forest. All enjoyed the scenery as of old—the beautiful, velvety, green lawns shaded by their magnificent oaks and magnolias; cool, shady dells carpeted with a rich growth of flowers; tall, white, sugar houses and long rows of cabins for the laborers; and lordly villas peering through groves of orange trees.

A pleasant surprise awaited them as they rounded at the wharf at Viamede. A great gathering of friends and relatives—not only from the immediate neighborhood but from that of their more northern homes. Edward Travilla and his family, Elsie Leland and hers, and Rose Croly with her little one were all there. It was a glad surprise to Violet, for her mother had not told her they had all been invited to spend the winter at Viamede and had accepted the invitation.

The cousins from Magnolia Hall, Torriswood, and the Parsonage cottage were all there. It seemed a joyful meeting to all—to none more so than to Chester and his sisters. It was their first meeting since his marriage, and they seemed glad to call Lucilla sister.

"You must be our guest at Torriswood, Lu, you and Brother Chester," said Maud, when greetings were over and the new arrivals were removing their hats in one of the dressing rooms.

"Thank you, Maud. Of course, we will spend a part—probably most—of our time with you," replied Lucilla. "I expect to have a delightful time both there and here."

"You shall there, if I can bring it about," laughed Maud. "I want you also, young Mrs. Raymond," she added in playful tones, turning to Evelyn. "You will come. Won't you?"

"Thank you, Maud. I think I shall," was Eva's pleased reply.

"You are wanted, too, Gracie," continued Maud. "And Dr. Harold is to be invited, and I hope will accept. He is a great favorite with us since he saved Dick's life."

"I think it entirely right that he should be," returned Gracie demurely, "and his presence will be no serious objection to me. In fact, as he is my physician, it might be very well to have him close at hand in case I should be taken suddenly ill."

"Very true," said Maud, bridling playfully. "Though if he were not there, Dr. Percival might possibly prove an efficient substitute."

There was a general laugh at that comment, and all hastened to join the rest of the company who were gathered upon the front veranda.

Elsie and Ned were there with their new pets, which seemed to be attracting a good deal of attention. Elsie was sitting by her mother's side with Tiny on her shoulder, and Ned stood near them with Tee-tee in his arms, stroking and patting him while he told how the little fellow had frightened him in his gambols about the yacht till, in trying to save him from falling into the sea, he had tumbled in himself.

"Very foolish of you to risk your life for me, little master," Tee-tee seemed to say, as Ned reached that part of his story.

Ned laughed, saying, "So you think, do you?"

"Oh, he can talk! He can talk!" cried several of the children in astonishment and delight, while their elders turned with amused, inquiring looks to Cousin Ronald, the known ventriloquist of the family connection.

"Yes, little master. So don't you do it ever again," seemed to come from Tee-tee's lips.

"No, indeed, I think I won't," laughed Ned.

"I can talk, too, quite as well as my brother can," seemed to come from Tiny's lips.

"Yes, so you can, my pretty pet," laughed Elsie, giving him an approving pat.

"Oh! They can both talk!" exclaimed several of the children.

"And speak good English, too, though they came from a land where it is not commonly spoken," laughed Chester.

"But we heard English on the yacht, and we can learn fast," was Tee-tee's answering remark.

"Especially when you get Cousin Ronald to help you," laughed Ned.

"There, Ned, I'm afraid you've let the cat out of the bag," laughed Lucilla.

"I don't see either cat or bag," sniffed Ned after an inquiring look around.

"Your sister means that you are letting out a secret," said his father.

"Oh, was I? I hope not," exclaimed the little fellow, looking rather crestfallen.

"How does Cousin Ronald help him?" asked one of the little cousins.

"I don't know," said Ned. "I couldn't do it."

The call to the supper table just at that moment saved Cousin Ronald the trouble of answering the inquiring looks directed at him.

After the meal, all resorted again to the veranda, and the little tee-tees, having had their supper in the kitchen, were again a source of amusement, especially to the children.

"Did the folks give you plenty to eat, Tee-tee?" asked Ned.

"All we wanted and very nice, too," the little fellow seemed to say in reply.

"And he ate like — like a hungry bear — a great deal more than I did," Tiny seemed to say.

"Well, I'm bigger than you," was Tee-tee's answering remark.

"And both of you are very, very little. Too little to eat much, I should think," laughed one of the children.

"I've heard that they put the best goods in the smallest packages," Tee-tee seemed to say. Then suddenly, he sprang out of Ned's arms, jumped over the veranda railing, ran swiftly across the lawn, and up an orange tree, Tiny leaving Elsie and racing after him.

"Oh, dear, dear! What shall we do? Will they ever come back?" cried Elsie, tears filling her eyes as she spoke.

"I think they will, daughter," said the captain, soothingly. "Do you forget that I told you they would run up the trees? You and Ned have been so kind to them — petted them and fed them so well that they'll be glad, I think, to continue in your care. But now, like children, they want a little fun, such as they have been accustomed to in their forest life."

That assurance comforted the young owners somewhat, and they chatted pleasantly with the other children until it was time for them to leave.

They kept watching the tee-tees frisking about in that tree and others on the lawn, hoping they would weary of their fun and come back to them. But they had not done so when the guests took their leave, nor when bedtime came. The captain comforted the children again with the hope that the tee-tees would finish their frolic and return the next day, which they did to the great joy of their young master and mistress.

Maud's invitation was accepted by all to whom she or Dick had given it. Magnolia Hall and the Parsonage claimed several of the others, and the rest were easily and well accommodated at Viamede. All felt themselves heartily welcome and greatly enjoyed their sojourn of some weeks in that hospitable neighborhood and among near and dear relatives.

Fortunately for Ned, his remark about Cousin Ronald helping the tee-tees with their talk did not have the bad effect that he feared, and the older friends did not explain. So, there was more fun of the same kind when the children were together and the kind old gentleman with them.

As the stay of Grandma Elsie and her party was to be short, there was a constant interchange of visits between them and the relatives resident in the neighborhood. Much to the delight of the children, the little tee-tees were on constant exhibition. Sometimes they were to be seen darting here and there over the lawn, running up and down the trees or springing from one to another, but often, to the greater pleasure of the young folks, they were on the veranda, chasing each other round and round or sitting on the shoulder of Elsie or Ned. If Cousin Ronald happened to be present, the two monkeys seemed to be in the mood for bits of conversation.

"I like this place, Tiny. Don't you?" Tee-tee seemed to ask one day, when they had just returned from a scamper over the lawn and up and down the trees.

"Yes, indeed!" was the reply. "It's nicer than that vessel we came in. Let's stay here."

"Oh, we can't. I heard the captain talking about going back, and they'll certainly want to take us along for the trip."

"But don't let us go. We can hide in the woods where they can't find us."

"I think not," laughed Elsie. "We value you too much not to hunt you up before we can go."

"Dear me! I'd take good care they didn't get a chance to play that game," exclaimed one of the cousins.

"I think the best plan will be to pet them so much that they won't be willing to be left behind," said Elsie.

"And that's what we'll do," said Ned.

Just then, there was an arrival of visitors from Torriswood, and that put a stop, for the time, to the chatter of the tee-tees.

Dr. Percival and his Maud with their guests from the north were of the party, and all remained until near bedtime that night, when they went away with the pleasant assurance that the whole connection at that time in the neighborhood would spend the following day with them in their lovely Torriswood home, should nothing occur to prevent.

Nothing did. The day was bright and beautiful, and not one of the relatives was missing from the pleasant gathering. To the joy of Elsie and Ned Raymond, not even the tee-tees were neglected in the invitation, and with some assistance from Cousin Ronald, they made a good deal of fun, for at least the younger part of the company.

The next day was spent by the same company at Magnolia Hall, and a few days later most of them gathered at the pretty Parsonage, where dwelt Cyril and Isadore Keith. Cyril was a much-loved and successful pastor and an excellent preacher, whose sermons were greatly enjoyed by those of the *Dolphin* party who were old enough to appreciate them.

The Parsonage and its grounds made a lovely home for the pastor, his wife, and the children with which Providence had blessed them. The family party held there, the last of the series, was found by all quite as enjoyable as any that had preceded it.

After that, the old pastimes of rides, drives, boating, and fishing excursions were resumed along with the quiet home pleasures and rambles through the woods and fields. They found they could not tear themselves away as quickly as they had intended when they planned to end their winter trip with a short visit to Viamede.

That neighborhood with its pleasant atmosphere and companionship was too delightful to be left until the increasing heat of the advancing spring made it less comfortable and healthful for them than their more northern homes.

The End

Invite little Elsie Dinsmore™ Doll Over to Play!

Breezy Point Treasures' Elsie Dinsmore™ Doll brings Martha Finley's character to life in this collectible eighteen-inch all-vinyl play doll produced in conjunction with Lloyd Middleton Dolls.

The Elsie Dinsmore™ Doll comes complete with authentic Antebellum clothing and a miniature Bible. This series of books emphasizes traditional family values so your and your child's character will be enriched as have millions since the 1800's.